CW00402393

TOOLS

OF THE

TRADE

CYNTHIA E. HURST

Silver and Simm Victorian Mysteries 1

© 2017 Cynthia E. Hurst
All rights reserved
Lilax Books

Cover photograph by Felix Mittermeier

Author's note: Witney in the 1860s was a thriving Oxfordshire market town, centered around the wool and blanket-making trades. This forms the background for the novel, but it is a work of fiction and the characters and situations portrayed here do not depict any actual persons, businesses or organizations. Various locations also have been fictionalized.

This book uses American spelling.

ONE

In years to come, Jacob Silver often wondered what would have happened if he had not been concentrating on his work so intently that his dinner had gone cold and he had not gone in search of the woman who provided his meals to see if she could re-heat it for him.

She wasn't in the kitchen as expected, so he went through the scullery and finally found her in the tiny garden at the rear of his house, leaning over the stone wall and deep in conversation with a domestic from the neighboring house. He had no doubt he was the topic under discussion, since both women stopped talking the moment they saw him approaching.

"I'll need the soup heated up again, Mrs Tucker," he said, making his tone slightly apologetic. "I'm afraid I was so absorbed in what I was doing that it's gone quite cold."

"And that's him all over," Mrs Tucker said to her companion, as if the subject of her comment weren't standing a few feet away. "So busy pokin' around at them little pieces of watches and clocks and jewelry and whatnot that he don't know if it's midday or midnight. All right, Mr Silver, I'll come in and hot it up for you in a minute."

"Thank you."

"Ever so polite, though," she added, lowering her voice. "Calls me missus and all, and he don't have to."

Jacob waited, knowing that she would keep gossiping and he'd be lucky to get a bowl of hot soup before supper if she

3

wasn't prodded along. He couldn't help sighing in resignation; it had been hard enough to find someone willing to work for him, let alone someone reasonably efficient. And despite her running commentary on his character and her occasional slovenliness, Mrs Tucker was a satisfactory housekeeper, coming in for a few hours each day to provide meals, do his washing and keep the house in a state of moderate cleanliness. These days, that was all he required.

Seeing that he wasn't going to leave, Mrs Tucker cast her eyes upward and waddled back inside. Jacob followed, his long legs taking one step to two of hers. She went straight to his workshop, picked up the offending bowl and took it into the kitchen, muttering all the while.

Jacob returned to his workbench, where he had been cleaning and repairing the gold pocket watch of a well-to-do customer. And froze, looking at the empty space on the bench where a few minutes earlier, the watch had been.

He looked around, as if expecting the missing watch to materialize. It was nowhere to be seen, disappeared as if spirited away. Had he taken it with him when he went to fetch Mrs Tucker? He thrust his hands into his pockets, but found nothing besides his own customary motley collection of objects.

Mrs Tucker emerged, carrying the bowl of soup and a plate holding a thick wedge of bread. She put it down in front of him and said pointedly, "Good and hot, this is."

"Yes, it smells delicious. Mrs Tucker, you haven't seen anyone come into the house, have you? Just now, I mean?"

"What sort of someone?"

"Anyone at all."

"No. Why?"

Jacob gestured toward workbench. "Mr Martyn's watch is gone. I was just working on it."

"Then it must be somewhere about. There's enough things here, you could lose something easy like." That was possibly true, given the collection of objects on the bench, but none of them were what he was looking for. And he wasn't apt to

4

overlook a fine gold watch, which had been sitting there with the cover opened, waiting for his touch.

"It was here when I went to find you. And now it's gone."

Mrs Tucker drew herself up, resembling a quail fluffing up its feathers.

"I hope you're not suggesting I had anything to do with it."

"No, I'm not. I simply don't understand how it could disappear." Jacob considered. "Well, I suppose I do, really. Someone must have looked in through the window, seen I wasn't in the room and come in and taken the watch. The door was on the latch."

He tried to keep his voice calm, but his mind was darting around frantically. The missing watch was an expensive one and a family heirloom as well, he'd been told. If it had been stolen, he would not only have to make up the cost to its owner – which, given his modest income, could take some time – but his reputation would suffer badly, something he could ill afford.

"Never mind, Mrs Tucker. It's a distinctive watch; so if someone tries to use it or pawn it, it will be noticed. That gives me a better chance of getting it back."

"And if you can't?"

"Then I'm afraid I shall owe Mr Martyn a great deal of money."

He could see her turning that thought over and coming to the logical conclusion – that he might no longer be able to afford her services. The alarm on her face was enough to convince him she had nothing to do with the theft.

"Oh, Mr Silver, I'm sure I hope it won't come to that."

"As do I," Jacob said grimly.

He ate the soup and bread without tasting it, trying to decide what action he should take. It seemed unlikely that a thief would take the watch to use as a timepiece, so it had been stolen for its value. That meant it would be have to be fenced or pawned at some point. Jacob could only hope that would be done locally and that the thief lacked the resources to take it to Oxford or worse, to London, where it would be nearly impossible to trace.

Accordingly, he pushed the empty bowl and plate to one side and went to the kitchen.

"I shall be out for a short while," he told Mrs Tucker. "The door will be locked and you're not to let anyone in."

"Even if they bring that watch back?"

Jacob shot her a suspicious glance, but she was serious.

"In that case, let them in and put the watch in a safe place. And thank you, the soup was excellent."

Mollified, she watched him take his hat and go out the door, locking it behind him. He walked briskly along Corn Street, aware of people watching him covertly. He was used to it now – the stares and whispered comments as the town's only Jewish resident passed. They were curious about him, naturally, and he'd had his share of verbal and occasionally physical abuse, but now there was also some sympathy in their attention.

When the typhoid epidemic had swept through Oxfordshire the previous year, it hadn't stopped to inquire as to the religion of its victims, and Jacob's wife and young daughter had been among them. He had been seriously ill himself, but had eventually recovered, at least physically. He felt the mental scars would never heal.

Corn Street ended at the crossroads dominated by the Buttercross, a landmark of the town since medieval days. He passed it, turned and walked along one of the gravel footpaths that bordered Church Green. The wide expanse of grass, lined on either side with houses and a handful of shops, was impressive and formed an approach for the imposing stone church at the far end. Jacob found the building aesthetically pleasing even if he didn't share the faith it represented, and normally he enjoyed looking at it. Today, however, it might as well have been a hovel for all the attention he gave it.

His goal was the police station, a new addition to the town. Policing outside London had been a rather haphazard affair until recently, and Jacob supposed the presence of a permanent police force in a market town like Witney – albeit a very small one consisting of a sergeant and a constable – meant its citizens felt more secure. But it didn't stop random opportunistic thefts, he thought, and smiled wryly.

He pushed the door open and stepped inside. Behind a wide wooden desk, the constable was laboriously writing in a ledger, his tongue clamped between his teeth. He looked up at Jacob's approach. Like many of the town's citizens, he knew him by sight and reputation, if not personally.

"Good afternoon, Mr Silver. Can I help you?"

"Good afternoon, Constable. Yes, I hope so." Jacob hesitated, torn between enlisting official help and admitting he had been careless enough to let a valuable watch be stolen. "I want to report a theft."

The constable pulled the ledger toward him and poised his pen over the page. "What's been stolen, then, sir?"

"A watch, one that I was repairing for a customer." Jacob gave a brief but complete description of the watch, although he stopped short of supplying the owner's name. He ended by saying, "I don't think the thief will be careless enough to display it in public, but it's always possible. More likely, it will be sold on for ready money."

The constable nodded. "Always a market for something like that, sir. We'll put the word out. Would you be offering a reward for its return, maybe?"

Jacob hadn't thought of that, but it wasn't a bad idea. "Yes, I'd be willing to."

"Fair enough. Word travels quickly amongst them that break the law, so I'll just drop a hint in the right places that Mr Silver'd be very glad of the watch's return. Very glad."

"Good. And you'll speak to the pawnbrokers as well? I'd see them myself, but it might have more impact coming from yourself."

"Yes, I'll do that, sir."

"Thank you, Constable. You've been very helpful. Good day to you."

When the station door had shut behind Jacob, the constable added a few words to his latest entry. He underlined one of them and muttered to himself, "Don't care what they say about him, at least he treats the police like we're human beings and that's more than some do."

Jacob retraced his steps back to Corn Street and his workshop, his heart sinking with every step. He didn't honestly expect the watch to be found and he wondered what on earth he could say to its prosperous owner. Of course he would have to make some kind of restitution, so he supposed he had better get to work on some of his other jobs. At least he would be able to collect his fee when those were finished. He was well aware the townspeople suspected he had a hidden fortune – they'd heard that Jews always had money, probably acquired through some complex and slightly unethical process. Unfortunately, the rumors were not true, at least not in his case.

He unlocked the door and settled himself at his workbench again. The silence from the rest of the house told him Mrs Tucker had finished her work for the day and departed. She would have left him something hot on the back of the stove for his supper, a portion of game pie, perhaps, or a piece of fish. Much as she sometimes irritated him, at least when she was there the sounds and smells of her housework helped him forget how alone he was, how much he missed Leah and Miriam.

He turned his attention to a malfunctioning carriage clock, wielding his instruments carefully as he probed its interior workings. It didn't take long to discover the problem, a bent tooth that was keeping the gear from turning smoothly. He straightened it, wound the clock and was rewarded by a steady ticking. If only all problems could be solved as easily, he thought, if only a dishonest person could be improved by straightening a small part of them.

He cleaned two other clocks – soot and greasy limestone dust were constant irritants in Cotswold houses – and put them aside to deliver to their owners. In a corner of his mind he also rehearsed the explanation he would give to Thomas Martyn for allowing his watch to be stolen. He didn't find it very satisfactory, so he doubted Martyn would, either. Martyn was an important man in a small town, although a pompous boor in Jacob's opinion, and he would probably enjoy making an example out of a Jewish watch repairer. The thought was not reassuring.

Eventually his stomach told him it was time to think about supper. He wandered back to the kitchen and found that Mrs Tucker had left him some stew, thick with vegetables and a few small pieces of meat. He hoped it wasn't pork – he had never been able to fully convince Mrs Tucker that no, he really didn't want some nice back bacon or a chop, no matter how appetizing it seemed to her. And although wild rabbits were plentiful in the fields around the town and hung by their furry legs outside the butcher's, they were also on his list of forbidden foods. It was next to impossible for Jacob to follow all the dietary restrictions his religion imposed, but he could almost always avoid those two.

He sniffed experimentally and decided the meat was poultry, possibly pheasant. He knew Mrs Tucker's eldest son frequently supplemented the family diet with pheasants poached from the nearby estate, and she sometimes brought part of one to use in Jacob's meals. At any rate, he wasn't in a position to complain, so he ate the stew with another piece of bread and a pot of tea, then put the dishes aside to be washed in the morning. He banked the fire, locked the front door, lit a candle and made his way upstairs to sleep in his lonely bed.

The following morning was cool and damp, and Jacob awoke to the sound of raindrops hitting the roof and window panes. He lay still for a moment, trying to remember why he felt so apprehensive, and then it all came back – the theft of the watch, his visit to the police station and his worry about the outcome.

He washed and dressed and went downstairs. It was eight o'clock and normally at this point, Mrs Tucker was there to prepare his breakfast and wash the dishes from the night before, but there was no sign of her. He stirred up the fire in the stove and put the kettle to heat for a cup of tea, expecting any minute to hear her rattling the door.

Instead, he heard a rapping noise and a tentative treble voice saying, "Mr Silver, sir?"

He turned and saw a small face looking in at the scullery window. Jacob went to open the door and recognized one of Mrs Tucker's several children.

"What is it, lad?"

"Our ma's poorly, sir, and I'm to tell you she won't be able to come do for you today."

"I'm sorry to hear that. What's the matter?"

Diagnostic skills were obviously beyond the child's ability. "Dunno, sir. She's just poorly."

"All right. Thank you for letting me know. Tell her I can manage until she's feeling better."

The boy ducked his head and ran off through the rain. Jacob poured the boiling water over the tea leaves, thinking this was just one more setback he didn't need. He used the remainder of the hot water to clean the dishes, then rummaged around until he located a dry linen towel and set them to dry on it.

There was half a loaf of bread in the cupboard, so he cut a slice and buttered it, washing it down with the tea. That took care of his immediate problem, but the larger one still loomed.

Back in the workshop, he bent over a necklace with a faulty clasp, looking at it through his glass while plying the metal with his calipers. He was so intent on the job that he didn't hear the door open and started abruptly when a voice said, "Mister?"

Jacob put down the glass and his tools and looked at the person who stood just inside the open door, as if poised to flee if necessary. He supposed it was a girl, judging by the bedraggled dress and shawl, but her light brown hair was cropped short and she was so thin he fancied he could nearly see her ribs. Large blue eyes, almost too big for her face, were fixed on him.

She didn't seem likely to be a potential customer, and he couldn't imagine what she wanted, unless Mrs Tucker had sent her to do some housework for him. So he said calmly, "Yes?"

"You Mr Silver?"

"Yes."

She shook back the shawl, which was wet from the rain. "I don't want to go to 'Stralia, mister."

Jacob blinked at this statement, which made little sense to him. He didn't particularly want to go to Australia, either, although the emigration office in Church Green was doing a roaring trade in ambitious would-be settlers who did.

"Fair enough," he replied.

"You don't understand," she said impatiently, digging into her skirt pocket. "Here, take it."

She held out her hand. In it was Martyn's gold pocket watch, a little grubbier than when Jacob had last seen it, but otherwise intact. Relief washed over him and he took the watch from her, setting it to one side.

"Where did you get this?"

She looked at him as if he were a simpleton. "From there," she said, pointing to his workbench.

"You mean you stole it."

She dipped her head. "You was in the other room. I didn't take nothin' else, honest."

"Why did you bring it back?"

She shifted from one foot to another and finally said in almost a whisper, "Heard talk you might pay to get it back."

"I see."

"And the constable was sniffin' around, and I was scared he'd find it and …"

"You didn't want to risk the boat," Jacob said, finishing her sentence. He could appreciate why she didn't want to be sent to Australia as a thief – even if she survived the voyage, her life would be extremely difficult and dangerous from that point onward. It was one thing to emigrate voluntarily, but criminals could expect a far worse experience.

She nodded.

"Well, since you returned the watch, I don't think you have to worry about that."

"And the money, mister?"

Jacob smiled. "What's your name, child?"

"I'm not a child," she said sharply. "I'm almost fourteen."

"I beg your pardon, miss. Your name?"

That brought something approaching a smile from her. "Sarah."

"And your surname?"

"Simm."

"And where do you live, Sarah?"

For the first time, it seemed she wasn't going to give him an answer. Jacob waited patiently and then repeated the question.

"The workhouse," she muttered. "Up Razor Hill."

Jacob knew the place, an establishment designed to provide the basics of existence for those who, for whatever reason, could not provide for themselves. That probably explained why the constable had paid a visit there – he would assume that poverty and dishonesty went hand in hand. It also explained the girl's cropped hair, which would have been shorn in the interest of controlling head lice.

"Have you been there long?"

"Since last winter. My ma died."

"And your father?"

"Been gone three years now."

She said it calmly, and Jacob felt a stab of sympathy.

"Typhoid?" he asked. It was a guess, but the disease was common enough. The poorer parts of the town with their rudimentary sanitation suffered the most, but even in the grander houses it was not unknown.

She nodded. "Ma and my little brother."

"I'm sorry, Sarah. It took my wife and daughter last year, too."

"Oh." Sarah looked straight at him. "I didn't know that."

"Well, so we have something in common. But if you're nearly fourteen, the workhouse will want you to leave soon, won't they? To go into service perhaps? I know some girls start working even younger."

"S'pose so."

"Do you often steal things?"

He expected her to be offended, but she said simply, "Not often. Usually food."

"You're very good at it, I must say. I didn't even hear you come in."

She nodded seriously, as if they were discussing her qualifications for a post. "I looked through the window and the room was empty. The door weren't locked. Thought I'd just take a chance."

"What would you have done if I'd come back in?"

"Scarpered, I expect." She gave him a shy smile and to his surprise, he found himself smiling back. He noticed that her speech veered back and forth between a broad Oxfordshire country accent and something more refined, and found himself wondering about her background prior to the workhouse.

"Can you read and write, Sarah?" he asked. It wasn't an idle question; many children from poor families had never been given the opportunity to learn.

"Course I can. And do my sums. I've had lessons."

"Good. And how about cooking and cleaning? Can you do that, too?"

"Yes, sir."

"So you should have no trouble finding a position, a clever girl like you."

He thought he detected a flicker of disappointment on her face, but before he could comment further, there was a brisk knock on the front door. Jacob went to open it, keeping a cautious eye on his visitor in case she had any ideas about reclaiming the watch while his back was turned. The constable he had spoken to the day before stood on the doorstep.

"Good morning, Mr Silver. May I have a word with you?"

"Certainly." He swung the door open and the constable came inside, looking around with frank curiosity, making Jacob wonder what he expected to see other than a cramped, dusty workplace in a very ordinary small terraced house. Sarah seemed to shrink into a corner, standing perfectly still, but the constable's gaze rested on her.

"You want to count the spoons after that one's been to visit," he said to Jacob.

Jacob didn't dare meet Sarah's eyes. He said mildly, "Oh? Why is that?"

"Goes through the stalls in the market, pinching anything not nailed down, she does. Or he does."

"Who's that?"

"Boy that's been seen doing the same thing. Daresay they're working together."

"But you haven't arrested either of them."

The constable looked both disgusted and chagrined. "Haven't been able to catch them with the goods. Oh, she's a sly one, sir."

"I see. Thank you for warning me. What did you want to see me about, Constable?"

"The watch that was stolen. I've put the word out to fences and spoken to the pawnshops."

Jacob took a second to weigh up the evidence and then without looking at Sarah, he put an apologetic expression on his face.

"I must apologize for putting you to so much trouble. The truth is, the watch has been found. I was planning to come by later this morning to tell you."

TWO

The constable's face was a picture of conflicting emotions, and Jacob thought he must have followed Sarah to the workshop door, hoping to catch her with the stolen watch or some other item.

He started to speak, changed his mind and settled for saying, "I'm glad to hear that, Mr Silver."

"Yes, I'm afraid I bothered you over nothing."

"Nothing? I thought you told me it had been stolen from your workshop."

Jacob could almost hear Sarah pleading with him not to turn her over to the constable. He debated whether she still qualified as a thief, considering she had returned the stolen property, even if she had hoped to profit in the end. On the other hand, he was going to have to explain her presence in the workshop unless he wanted to be suspected of fencing stolen goods himself.

"Yes, I very foolishly forgot I had taken it to another room and assumed it had been stolen." He gestured to the workbench. "There it is, as you can see."

"And the girl? Why is she here?"

"I am considering taking on someone to help my housekeeper with the heavier household chores. She has applied for the position."

The constable looked from Jacob to Sarah in frank disbelief. He said reluctantly, "Very well. The matter is closed, then?"

"Yes. Thank you for your help."

As the door closed behind the constable, Sarah let her breath out with a soft whistle.

"Ta, Mr Silver." She turned toward the door.

"Wait."

"Yes?"

"I thought you were looking for a reward."

"I reckon you don't owe me nothing now. You could have shopped me and you didn't."

"And you could have kept the watch and landed me in a great deal of trouble. That balances the books, I think. Do you want to go into service?"

She made a face. "No, but I got no choice, do I?"

He supposed she was right. The alternatives for a girl in her situation might be considerably worse – back-breaking work in one of the town's blanket or glove factories if she was lucky, begging or prostitution if she wasn't.

"I was quite serious, you know, about the position I mentioned to the constable," he said. Sarah's eyebrows went up and he continued, "Mrs Tucker is ill at the moment, and the heavy washing and scrubbing is difficult for her to manage at the best of times. You would be a great help to her, I think. Would you be interested?"

Her blue eyes studied him, then surveyed the workshop doubtfully.

"Might be. Would I stop here?"

"There's a box room upstairs you could sleep in. It was my daughter's nursery and has a bed in it. It's small, but I imagine it would be an improvement on the workhouse. Unless you have some family, some other place to go."

She shook her head and he could see her weighing up the offer, wondering if he had any ulterior motive. He didn't blame her; employers sometimes did, and normally it would have been a wife or daughter who would have been responsible for hiring

16

servants and managing the household. That made him think of Leah and he felt the familiar pang of grief. He hurried on, aware that he didn't even know what sort of pay he should be offering, although he had an idea that if she lived in, he would only be expected to provide her with enough money to cover her clothing costs and personal items like soap.

"I'm afraid I don't know what I should be paying you, but you can eat and sleep here, which should be worth something. If you're willing, shall we try it for a while and see what you think?"

A smile broke across her face. "Them up at the workhouse, they say you're odd," she said. "A heretic, they call you. I don't rightly know what that means, but you've not done me any harm. I haven't got any other family and I'd rather work here than some places I've heard about. Some of 'em want you to sleep on the kitchen floor, so a whole box room to myself, with a bed ..."

"Good," Jacob said. "Then that's settled."

Sarah arrived at the house that afternoon, her worldly possessions contained in a shabby bag slung over her shoulder, lugging it up the stairs to the small room where she would sleep. Jacob was thankful now that he hadn't removed the bed in the room after Miriam's death, the one she would have used when she was a little older. Sarah made no comment, so he assumed it would suit her, and left her to get settled. He didn't dare think about what Mrs Tucker would say when she discovered he had installed a young woman in the box room, but he had been entirely serious about her role in the household.

When she came back down, he made this clear by giving her a few coins and sending her to the market to buy food for the evening meal.

"A cabbage, three or four carrots and the freshest piece of fish you can find. Then come straight back."

"Yes, sir."

"And I'll expect you to return any money not spent."

"Yes, sir."

"Sarah."

"Yes?"

"What did they say at the workhouse when you told them you were coming here?"

"Nothing, 'cause I didn't say where I was going. They were just glad to see the back of me, I reckon."

That was entirely possible, Jacob thought. She was far too intelligent to blindly obey the workhouse rules, which were outwardly benevolent but all designed to remind the occupants of their lowly place in society.

"It's probably just as well you didn't tell them," he agreed. "Oh, and Sarah."

"Yes, sir?"

"Don't mention anything about that watch to anyone."

"I ain't a gossip, Mr Silver."

"I'm delighted to hear that. On your way, now."

She went off in the direction of the market, Mrs Tucker's basket over one arm, and Jacob took a close look at the watch Sarah had returned. He opened the cover to check that it was indeed the correct one, engraved with the initials TGM and a date, 1815. Martyn hadn't supplied details, those being no concern of a mere workman, but given the date, Jacob supposed the watch had been presented following the battle of Waterloo to Martyn's father, or perhaps grandfather. It was a fine watch, and he wasn't surprised it had become a valued family heirloom.

At the moment it looked rather dirty and there were a few tiny scratches, but those could be dealt with easily. Heaving a sigh of relief that he didn't have to explain its loss to Thomas Martyn, Jacob checked the workings to make sure his repairs and cleaning of the previous few days hadn't been undone during Sarah's possession. It seemed to be in perfect order, so he set to work polishing the scratches out of the cover.

He had been working for nearly an hour when it occurred to him she was taking a long time conducting her business at the market, which was only a few streets away. He had no doubt that she was a shrewd bargainer, so perhaps that explained it, since the walk itself should have taken her no more than five or six minutes each direction. Or she might have encountered someone she knew and despite her claim, stopped to chat for a while, telling them about her new position.

There was no earthly reason why he should feel concern over the girl, who had so nearly caused a crisis in his life, but that in itself might be the explanation – she could have ruined his livelihood and perhaps more, but she hadn't. Admittedly she had returned the stolen watch in an effort to save herself, but still …

He was more relieved than he wanted to admit when the door opened a few minutes later and Sarah nearly flew into the room.

"What's the matter?" he asked her.

She closed the door and leaned against it, panting as if she'd run the entire distance from the market to the house. He waited patiently.

"Are you all right?"

She nodded.

"So what's wrong?"

"That watch."

"This one?" He indicated Martyn's watch, now polished to a fine sheen.

"Yes."

"What about it?"

"That constable. The one who was here."

Jacob nodded.

"He's been sayin' you just pretended to lose the watch so as the owner would put up a reward for it and you'd get the money."

Jacob took a minute to think about it and then said, "But that's nonsense. Mr Martyn didn't even know the watch went missing for a while and besides, I was the one who was going to offer a reward for its return."

"And who are people going to believe, Mr Silver, you or the constable?"

19

"Him, I suppose. How do you know this, Sarah?"

She shuffled her feet. "I know lots of people. Not the sort you do, I expect."

"I see." Jacob decided not to press for details. "And why was the constable sharing this piece of information with them?"

"He wasn't. They heard him tellin' somebody."

"Just one somebody?"

"Think so."

"In that case, we won't worry too much. Not yet, at least. Now get yourself into the kitchen, Sarah, and let's see how you are at cooking supper. Fish, potatoes, cabbage and carrots, enough for both of us. Can you do that?"

"Yes, sir. My ma taught me to cook and I worked in the kitchen at the workhouse."

"Good. You'd best get started, then."

She still hesitated and he said, "What is it?"

"That Mr Martyn. Is that his watch?"

"Yes."

"Mr Thomas Martyn what lives in Church Green?"

"Yes. What about him?"

The words came out in a rush. "I know about him 'cause my ma was in service there 'fore she and my pa were married, and after Pa died she thought as he might help her out, maybe take her back so she wouldn't have to go into the workhouse."

"But obviously he didn't."

"No, the miserable ..." She stopped, angrily brushing tears from her eyes. "Said he had no responsibility for her and her brats."

"Ah. I see." On one hand, Jacob could see that taking on a servant with two young children was a different proposition than engaging an unmarried or widowed woman. On the other hand, it wouldn't have hurt Martyn to let go of a few coins each month to help out someone who had given him good service. He decided to add a little to the amount he had planned to charge the man for the repair of his watch as a sort of retroactive punishment for his stinginess.

Sarah was watching him, as if expecting him to react to her comments, perhaps even defend Martyn's actions. He imagined that she hadn't dared complain about Martyn while she was in the workhouse, but that didn't mean she hadn't nursed her resentment privately.

"I will return Mr Martyn's watch to him tomorrow," he said. "And that will be the end of it, I think. If he has his watch back, then there's no question of it being stolen. By anyone, or by no one, for that matter."

Sarah still looked skeptical, but she brushed past him to take the basket of food into the kitchen.

"If you need to know where anything is, just ask me," Jacob called after her.

"Ta, Mr Silver."

He went back to work, keeping one ear on the sounds coming from the kitchen. Sarah was obviously acquainting herself with its facilities, since he heard plates and bowls being moved around, the gurgle of water in the kettle and the clunk of the iron stove door as she stirred up the fire.

Jacob hoped she had been telling the truth about her ability to cook, and was relieved when eventually the odor of fried fish and cabbage wafted out into the workshop. He put the clock he was repairing to one side and went into the kitchen.

Sarah was standing at the stove, her face damp from the steam rising from the two saucepans. A piece of fish sizzled in the frying pan beside them.

"It's almost done, sir," she said.

"Good. I'll get the plates and cutlery." He smiled at her astonished expression. "Don't worry. It's just the two of us, so we won't stand on ceremony."

"You want me to eat in here with you?" Her blue eyes were wide.

"Where else would you go? You need to eat somewhere and this isn't exactly Blenheim Palace. I don't have a servants' hall and I'm not about to make you stand in the scullery or banish you to the garden."

Jacob took two clean plates from the cupboard and placed them on the table, while Sarah pondered his words. He put a knife, fork and spoon by each one.

"There. Let's see how good a cook you are."

Sarah grinned impishly at him and divided the food between the two plates, one considerably fuller than the other, and placed them on the pine table. She sat down cautiously in the chair opposite him, folded her hands and waited. Jacob was puzzled, wondering if she expected him to take the lead in eating, and then realized she was waiting for him to recite a blessing of some sort.

"In my faith, we usually give thanks after the meal, not before it," he told her. "But you go ahead, if you want to."

Her eyes widened again. She bowed her head, mumbled a prayer under her breath, and after a last curious glance at him, bent over her supper.

Jacob had never seen a plate emptied so quickly. He deduced she had been very hungry, and that the modest meal was probably the biggest one she had eaten for months, perhaps years. It was no wonder her clothes seemed to hang on her, as if intended for someone larger.

He ate his own supper in a more leisurely fashion, quietly gave thanks for the food received, and smiled as Sarah bustled around, taking the dishes to the stone sink in the scullery and washing them. When she had finished, she hung the linen towel neatly on the rack and came back into the kitchen.

"Will there be anything else, Mr Silver?"

"Not at the moment, Sarah, thank you. That was a very good meal."

"Ta. Will Mrs Tucker be here tomorrow?"

"I don't know. I'll just have to wait and see. Why?"

"I can do the washing if she doesn't come. And if she does …" Sarah's voice trailed off.

"What?"

"What'll she think about me being here, Mr Silver? Will she be cross?"

Jacob had a feeling that Mrs Tucker would probably suspect him of disreputable motives in installing a girl of thirteen in the house, not because she had any evidence, but because it made a better piece of gossip. On the other hand, he imagined he rated so low in the estimation of most of his fellow citizens that Sarah's residency could hardly harm his reputation.

"That will depend, I think, on how helpful you are to her," he said. "But in any case, I make the decisions here. As far as I am concerned, you are now part of this household."

"Ta, Mr Silver."

An unwelcome thought flitted across Jacob's mind as he watched her look around the kitchen. If she was in the house on a permanent basis, he wanted to be sure she wasn't tempted to fall back into her old ways.

"Sarah, that constable mentioned a boy, someone you know? He said the two of you stole from the market stalls. There will be no stealing in this household. If you need something, ask me. And tell your young friend as well."

Sarah looked up at him and a smile spread across her face.

"There's no boy," she said. "That was me, wearin' some trousers and boots and an old jacket, and rubbin' a little dirt on my face and hands. Foolish man, couldn't tell the difference. He never said he saw the two of us at the same time, did he?"

Jacob stared at her for a minute, taking in the cropped hair and the figure so slender that it could be easily mistaken for a boy's. Then he burst out laughing, astonished to realize it was the first time since Leah and Miriam's deaths that he had done so.

"I see," he said, when he had caught his breath. "That was clever of you, but all the same, Sarah, your thieving days are over. Do you understand me?"

"Course I do," she said. She turned back to the sink, and Jacob had to strain to hear her words. "I don't steal from them who've been good to me, anyways. So you got nothing to worry about."

THREE

The following morning, Jacob rose early, not only because he had a busy day ahead of him, but also because he wanted to be sure the new addition to the household hadn't vanished during the night. And in spite of her assurances, he wouldn't have been surprised to find a few silver spoons or a watch had disappeared along with her.

So he washed, shaved and dressed more quickly than usual, listening to catch any early morning sounds in the kitchen. A quick glance in the looking glass showed his reflection, a man not yet thirty, but with worry and sorrow etched on his thin face. His hair was thick and dark, his eyes a clear gray under dark brows. There were few obvious outward signs of his Jewish heritage, and yet somehow everyone knew he was different. A heretic, one who refused to work on Saturdays and instead spent his Sundays repairing clocks and watches instead of in more suitably reverent activities. He'd always found it ironic that it was acceptable for the factory workers to toil on Sunday while he was pilloried for doing the same.

As he finished dressing, Jacob heard familiar noises in the kitchen – familiar, that is, to the days when Leah had risen early and prepared him a cup of tea to be drunk as soon as he came downstairs. Mrs Tucker tended to arrive later, so that he now brewed his own and frequently was on his second or third cup by the time she got there.

But this morning he could hear the gurgle of water, the sound of the fire being poked into life and then the scent of strong tea. Definitely not Mrs Tucker, so that meant Sarah was still there and going about her work. He grimaced at his reflection and went down the narrow stairs and into the kitchen.

She was standing by the stove, a worried expression on her face.

"Good morning, Sarah," Jacob said. "Is something wrong?"

"Don't rightly know," she said, then added politely, "Morning, Mr Silver."

"That tea smells good," he said. "Shall we have a cup?"

"Oh, arr," she said, and he smiled. The phrase was a local one, used for expressing anything from agreement to doubt, depending on the inflection. She filled his cup, placed it on the table, and then after a moment of hesitation, poured another one for herself.

"I didn't know what you was wanting for breakfast," she said, frowning. "Don't seem to be any bacon or kippers or anything, and I know gentlemen like those."

"I don't eat bacon, although I confess I'm partial to the occasional kipper," Jacob said. "For today, though, a round of toast will be enough."

He might have added that few people classified him as a gentleman, but Sarah was already at the stove, cutting a slice of bread from the loaf. She deftly turned it over the fire until it was toasted to a golden brown and slid it onto a plate. The pot of butter, he noted, was already on the table.

"Make some for yourself as well," he said, reaching for the butter, and after a quick sideways glance, she obeyed.

They settled down to eat in a comfortable silence. Jacob marveled at how easily she fit into his household and tried to suppress the suspicion that she had the ability to take on any characteristics as needed, with an eye to petty crime. He reminded himself that she could have cleared out his workshop, including several valuable watches, during the night if she'd wanted to, and then disappeared. But instead, she was sitting at his table, eating his bread and drinking his tea. He decided it was a good omen.

Jacob finished the toast, refilled his cup and took it into his workshop, while Sarah cleared the crockery. He put Thomas Martyn's watch carefully into a small cloth bag, ready to deliver to its owner, and looked around to decide what task to start on next. He chose a carriage clock and turned it over, ready to remove the back, when a clamor from the back of the house made him jump.

"You, girl, what are you doing in Mr Silver's house?"

The furious voice belonged to Mrs Tucker, obviously recovered from her ailment. Jacob stood up and started toward the kitchen, then stopped, curious to hear what Sarah would say.

"I'm washing the crockery, missus."

"Who told you to do that? Does Mr Silver know you're here?"

"Course he does." Sarah sounded amused. "He's just finished his breakfast, hasn't he? Didn't want to wait all morning for it. He's got work to do. And I've got to scrub that table, too. Hasn't been done properly for ages, what I can see."

A sputtering noise followed, which Jacob identified as Mrs Tucker's response to the slur on her cleaning standards, then a crash as something shattered against the stone slabs of the scullery floor.

"Oo, you shouldn't have done that," Sarah said. "Breaking a cup? Now Mr Silver will be cross, for sure."

"And how would you know, you hussy? Me, I've been doing for him ever since his wife and little daughter were taken, poor man. I know him better than you do, for sure." A pause, which Jacob felt was full of unspoken innuendo. "Unless you know him some other way."

There was another crash, which Jacob could only hope wasn't anything irreplaceable, followed by a shriek. He decided it was time to intervene. He went to the door and looked through.

The two combatants were concentrating so hard on each other that neither noticed his approach. Sarah had her back to the stone sink, her fists clenched around a wet cloth. Mrs Tucker, who probably outweighed her by at least three stone, stood in the doorway, arms akimbo. The front of her dress was soaked with water and the remains of a teacup and saucer were scattered between them on the floor.

"What's going on here?" he inquired mildly.

"Who's she?" Mrs Tucker demanded.

"Her name's Sarah. I've engaged her to help you with the housework."

"That little thing? She'll be no help to me. No more meat on her than a ha'penny rabbit."

Sarah drew herself up to her full height, which Jacob estimated at a little over five feet. She reminded him of a furious kitten squaring up to a snarling bulldog.

Before she could speak, he said, "I've heard you say some of the work is becoming too difficult for you, Mrs Tucker. I'm sure Sarah will be a great help. I've already discovered she's quite a good cook."

"And she's good at other things, too, no doubt," Mrs Tucker said. "Well, I'm not stoppin' in a household where there's that sort of goings-on. I'm a respectable woman. You can have her, and good luck to you."

Jacob lifted his eyebrows, remembering it had been only two days earlier she had been worried about the possibility of losing her post if he couldn't afford to pay her. Obviously, her viewpoint had shifted, or perhaps she simply felt obliged to get her moral stance on record.

"Very well, if that's how you feel," he said. "But I'm not dismissing you. If you change your mind, you are welcome to return."

She turned and stamped out of the scullery, pulling her shawl across the wet dress. Jacob heard her angry footsteps going across the small garden and fading away down the lane that ran behind the terraced houses.

Sarah stood still, her blue eyes wide.

"I didn't say nothing to her, honest, Mr Silver. She just come stormin' in here and started having a go at me."

"I know. I heard you, as did half the street, I expect. Did you hit her with the wet cloth?"

Sarah looked down as if she'd forgotten she was holding it. "'Fraid so, Mr Silver. I'm sorry. Do you want me to go?"

"No, because then I'd be worse off than I was before, with no help at all. Besides, Mrs Tucker may come back when she's calmed down."

"And if she don't?"

"Then we'll have to manage without her. But I think she'll be back."

She nodded and then said, "Mr Silver?"

"Yes?"

"That table, it do need scrubbing. Maybe she can't see so good anymore."

"It's possible."

They both looked toward the pine table, which indeed had grubby areas where food or drink had been spilled and not thoroughly cleaned.

"Mr Silver?"

"Yes?"

"I don't reckon you was planning anything like what she said you was."

Jacob took a moment to untangle the sentence. "No, of course I'm not."

She gave him a shy smile and said, "Ta. There's some that do, you know."

"Yes, I know. But Sarah, you must learn to think before you act. A wet cloth has hurt nothing but her pride, but if it had been something else …"

Sarah nodded soberly. "I won't do it again."

"Very well. Did you break the cup and saucer?"

"No, sir, not exactly. They fell off the table."

"How did that happen?"

"Not sure, sir. Could have happened when she tried to grab my apron and I backed off."

Jacob's mouth twitched as he tried to keep his face serious. It wouldn't do to encourage his new domestic help to think she could get away with brawling in the scullery, or for that matter, telling minor falsehoods.

"Clear the pieces up, Sarah, and then get on with your cleaning. I've got my own work to see to, and later on, I'll take Mr Martyn's watch to him and you can do the marketing."

He went back to the workshop, listening with half his attention to the sounds of washing and scrubbing. Obviously Sarah was taking out her irritation on the pine table. He cleaned the carriage clock and set it to going again, listening with a sense of satisfaction to the regular ticking. Repairing jewelry was all very well, but necklaces and bracelets were mostly for show and his conservative soul shrank from such ostentatious displays. A fine clock or watch, on the other hand, was both useful and ornamental, and they were often family heirlooms as well.

That reminded him of his morning's errand and he picked up the bag containing the watch, tucking it into his pocket. He took his coat and hat from the peg and looked into the kitchen, where Sarah was just hanging up her apron and reaching for her shawl.

"See, Mr Silver? That table come up real good."

The pine table was indeed glistening, the grain clear. Jacob nodded.

"You've done very well. If you're ready to go to the market, shall we walk together?"

Sarah's eyes grew wide.

"Would that be proper, Mr Silver?"

"I very much doubt it. Shall we go?"

She grinned at him and he found himself smiling back. "Yes, sir."

Sarah put the marketing basket over her arm, and Jacob handed her the money she would need for her purchases. There were only a few shops willing to extend credit to a Jew, and most of them refused to deliver to his house, but the market stallholders would always sell to him for ready cash, and he never complained.

They went out the front door and walked side by side along Corn Street, Jacob amused at the covert glances being thrown their way by passers-by and cart drivers. He was fully aware that accompanying one's housemaid to town was simply not done, but it seemed absurd that they should be walking in the same direction at the same time and each pretending the other didn't exist.

He suspected Sarah felt the same. After her first shocked reaction, she had fallen into step beside him, hurrying a little to keep up with his longer strides. Neither of them indulged in any casual conversation as they walked; there would be gossip enough without giving any more cause for speculation.

They reached the Buttercross and Jacob said, "You might see about getting another trout, if they've got some in fresh today. That was very good, the one you cooked last night."

"Yes, sir. Thank you, sir."

"And take your time; I'll likely be a while with Mr Martyn."

"Yes, sir."

Jacob noted with amusement that he hadn't had to explain his comment. Sarah would know there was probably only one key to the front door of his house and he wasn't about to relinquish it to her. There were two keys to the scullery door in the rear, but Mrs Tucker had the spare one and again, he was somewhat reluctant about Sarah being in the house without his presence. An ordinary housemaid wouldn't have left the house at all during the day unless an emergency arose, but Sarah was clearly not ordinary. Jacob batted aside the notion that lock-picking might be among her various skills.

Sarah turned left to go to the market and Jacob turned right, walking along Church Green toward the imposing house that was the home of Thomas Martyn. Like most of the other houses lining the broad green, it was built of solid cream and gray

Oxfordshire limestone, its three stories topped with a roof of Stonesfield slates.

Martyn's family had made their money in wool, like many of Witney's other prosperous citizens, although Jacob was a little vague on what exactly the current Thomas Martyn did to occupy his days. There was an office, he knew, adjacent to the large blanket factory established by the man's father, and rumor had it that Martyn actually made an occasional personal appearance at the factory that kept him and his family in style.

On the previous occasion when he had called, Martyn had seemed abstracted, as though worrying about whether the demand for fine woolen blankets and broadcloth would continue. Or perhaps it had been something more personal, which he certainly would not have discussed with a mere watch repairer. Jacob shrugged his shoulders and set his steps toward the tradesmen's entrance.

He expected to have to wait a while before Martyn condescended to receive him, assuming he was there, or possibly he would be fobbed off on another member of the household. So he wasn't surprised to be told to wait in a drafty room while it was determined whether Mr Martyn was at home and would see him. Or Martyn might genuinely not be at home and could be found at his place of business or elsewhere. Jacob rested his hands on his knees and waited.

He spent his time glancing around the room, a parlor of some sort, he decided, but not the one used for receiving the better class of visitors. The furniture was adequate but a little shabby, and the oriental carpet was worn. The framed pictures on the walls were banal landscapes which could have depicted any rural part of England. A few small faded squares on the wallpaper showed where pictures had previously hung but had been removed altogether. Jacob deduced that this room was where objects were put that had seen better days or were not at all cherished by the family. He fingered the bag which held the watch. That, at least, was an heirloom worth treasuring.

His musings were brought to a close when the door opened suddenly, as if someone had given it a sharp push from the other side. A young man came into the room – no, *staggered* into the room would be a better description, Jacob thought. He was probably around thirty years old, expensively dressed and shod, so undoubtedly a member of the family, but his florid face seemed to droop, as if he had either had too much drink or not enough sleep. He stared at Jacob, who stood up and nodded to him politely.

"Good morning, sir."

The man focused with some difficulty, as if trying to reconcile Jacob's lowly tradesman status with the fine fabric and expert tailoring of his wool coat.

"Who the devil are you?"

"My name is Jacob Silver. I've come to deliver a watch that I've repaired. Your father's, perhaps?"

The young man pulled himself together. "Yes. Yes. My father's watch. Or rather, my grandfather's. The one he received after Waterloo."

"Yes, sir." Jacob debated whether to give the watch to him and decided against it. There was something about him, an unnatural gleam in his eyes that told him the man was not to be trusted, even if he was the son of the house.

He knew he had made the correct decision when the door opened again and Thomas Martyn came in, a solidly built man in his mid-fifties, with what seemed to be a permanent scowl on his countenance. He stopped abruptly upon seeing his son and then said, "Nathaniel, you won't be needed here."

It was clearly a dismissal. Nathaniel's eyes locked on Martyn's for a moment and then he turned and went out, closing the door behind him. Jacob felt a mingling of curiosity and embarrassment at witnessing such an awkward moment, and to cover it, he took the bag from his coat pocket.

"My son, Nathaniel," Martyn said. He seemed about to elaborate on the bare statement, but changed his mind.

"Here is your watch, Mr Martyn," Jacob said, drawing it from the bag. "I've cleaned and repaired it." *And lost it and found it again*, he added silently. "I hope you find it to your satisfaction."

Martyn took the watch and examined it closely. He held it to his ear, lowered it and opened the lid.

"It seems to be running well," he said.

"Yes, sir. If I may say so, sir, it's a very fine watch and I believe you said it is also a family heirloom."

"Yes, my father was at Waterloo," Martyn said. "You no doubt observed the date engraved inside the cover whilst you were working on it. His father presented him with the watch on his return."

Jacob wondered if he should comment on the unsuitability of such a treasure being passed down to Nathaniel, but was saved the trouble when Martyn said, "Do you have a son, Silver?"

"No, sir. I had a small daughter, but she died of the typhoid."

"My elder son, Frederick, also, some years ago. Only nineteen years old and just beginning to take a real interest in the family business. Such a waste. Would that Nathaniel …"

Martyn stopped abruptly, perhaps realizing he was discussing personal matters with a distinctly inferior person. He shook his head just slightly and asked, "Did you learn your trade from your father?"

"No, sir. My father was a tailor, and my older brother followed him in that trade, but I was apprenticed to a silversmith as a lad. He also repaired clocks and watches. I was never very artistic, so I was put to work cleaning the clocks and eventually, to repairing them."

When Martyn didn't reply immediately, he added, "I enjoy my work, actually, finding out why a clock or watch isn't running properly and setting it right."

"I wish my son was interested in something as useful," Martyn said, a trace of bitterness creeping into his voice. "Very well, Silver. Send me your bill and it will be paid."

Jacob understood he was being dismissed. "Yes, sir. Good day to you."

He waited to be ushered out the tradesmen's entrance and emerged into Church Green again. He turned to look back at the handsome house. In the front parlor, a curtain twitched, and as Jacob moved away, he caught a glimpse of Nathaniel Martyn, staring after him.

FOUR

For a fortnight or more after the return of Thomas Martyn's watch, life went on calmly in Jacob's household. The bill sent to Martyn was paid promptly and in full, including the extra two shillings Jacob had charged for the insult to Sarah's mother. And as predicted, Mrs Tucker made a reappearance, ostensibly to instruct Sarah in how to cook and clean properly, but Jacob suspected she was more interested in making sure he – or Sarah – weren't overstepping any moral boundaries.

He smiled at the thought. In many ways, Sarah was the sort of girl he had hoped his daughter would become – intelligent, loyal and hard-working, with an appealing scrappiness. Of course, Miriam would have had some advantages Sarah hadn't, but then Sarah would never have to put up with the prejudice that came with being Jewish.

She didn't seem to have any reservations about working for the town's pariah, and made no comment when he told her that she was free to attend church on Sunday, but that it was a normal working day for him. His day of rest, he explained, was Saturday, a fact she accepted readily, albeit with slightly raised eyebrows.

Jacob was also pleased to find that with or without Mrs Tucker's guidance, she was capable of turning out tasty meals and rapidly learning to cope with his dietary requirements.

"I can't see as how you can't eat bacon or a nice bit of rabbit pie," she said one evening. It wasn't a complaint, simply a comment, and Jacob found himself trying to explain how the dietary laws had originated. He was thankful he hadn't attempted to keep a kosher kitchen after Leah's death; it had been difficult enough to train Mrs Tucker to avoid the foods he wouldn't eat. Sarah listened intently and he had the impression she was soaking up information like a sponge.

"Still don't make sense to me," she said, then corrected herself. "It still *doesn't* make sense to me."

"Sometimes things don't make sense, but we still have to do them," Jacob said, amused that she was starting to pick up his speech patterns. He hadn't had much formal education himself, but his father had been quick to criticize when his children's grammar or diction had been less than perfect. A well-constructed sentence had been as important to him as a perfectly fitted coat or pair of trousers.

"But no one would know if you didn't."

"I would know."

She nodded thoughtfully, then with one of her lightning-quick changes of subject, said, "It's my birthday tomorrow, Mr Silver."

"Then I shall wish you many happy returns. Tomorrow, that is."

He made a mental note of the date, wondering if she was hinting that she might be given some sort of recognition or even a gift. Housemaids would not expect anything from the master of the house in the ordinary course of events, but Jacob had almost stopped thinking of her as a housemaid. She filled that role, to be sure, but in the course of a few days, she had also become a companion, almost a friend.

Sarah never spoke much about her life before the workhouse, although he knew her father had been a farm laborer and her mother, of course, had been a housemaid in the Martyns' household. Jacob gathered from a few unguarded comments that the family had been poor, and Sarah had only been able to attend lessons for a few years, probably at one of the ragged schools that catered to the less fortunate. Then the typhoid had come, taking first her father, followed three years later by her mother and younger brother. It was a sad story, but not an uncommon one.

Still, she had emerged from it with self-respect and resilience, even if she had stooped to a few dishonest acts along the way. He doubted if he would have acted any differently under the circumstances, and of course a girl had obstacles placed in her way that a boy of the same age would never have to face. Among other things, at fourteen, a girl – even a housemaid – would start thinking ahead to marriage and would begin to behave accordingly.

He cast a sideways glance at Sarah, wondering if she harbored any ideas or plans for the future. She always struck him as someone who lived for the moment, as evidenced by the way she had accepted his offer of employment and moved into his house. That move had dealt with her immediate problems; she would evaluate the situation later and change it if necessary. He was acutely aware she might have trouble finding another post after being employed by him, but she either hadn't considered this or hadn't thought it important.

As if following his thoughts, she said, "I'd have been out on the street if you hadn't taken me in, Mr Silver, so it's a good thing I nicked that watch, wasn't it?"

Jacob tried to keep from smiling. "It was wrong of you to steal it," he reminded her, "but at least you returned it."

They were sitting in the kitchen, as usual. Because Jacob used his largest room as his workshop, and the parlor was dim and poky, he normally sat at the kitchen table after the evening meal, sipping a cup of tea and unwinding from the day's work. If he had an on-going project that needed to be finished, he might return to the workshop, but it was more common for him to light the lamps and read a book at the table while Sarah whisked about tending to her evening chores.

Once she was finished, she would join him for an hour or so of conversation, often combining this with sewing or mending as she was doing this evening, turning a collar on one of his well-worn shirts. He was certain that in a better regulated household, Sarah would have been banished to the scullery or her room to carry out this work, but he enjoyed her company and was entertained by her perspective on life, so different from his own. He still missed Leah and Miriam, but the raw pain of loss was lessening to a dull ache, thanks in large part to Sarah's cheerful chatter.

She neatly snipped off the last thread and held the shirt up for his inspection.

"Looks as good as new, don't it, Mr Silver?"

"Yes, it does. You've done a fine job, Sarah."

She folded the shirt carefully and added it to the pile of clothing. She took up the next item to be dealt with, a dress of plain dark material that, as far as Jacob could tell, was the only other one she owned besides the one she was wearing.

He didn't see anything on it that needed mending and wondered if she was subtly hinting that she needed more clothing. Although she had only been in the house for a fortnight, her thin frame was already starting to fill out a bit and her shorn hair was beginning to grow. She would be quite attractive someday, he realized, which meant he would have to set some boundaries as to male followers. But hopefully, that day would be some way off.

He was thinking of how to frame a question tactfully about her clothing needs, when a loud tattoo of knocks on the front door made them both start. Jacob rose from his chair and went down the short hallway to the door, opening it only a crack. It wouldn't be the first time young men with too much drink inside them had thought it would be amusing to annoy the town's only Jew.

But the doorstep was occupied by a completely unexpected visitor. Thomas Martyn stood there, not seeming to notice the raindrops dripping from his hat and running down his coat.

Jacob peered over his shoulder through the darkness, expecting to see a carriage waiting in Corn Street, but there was none. And on reflection, he realized Martyn would have sent a servant to the door if he had arrived in style, not come himself.

"Good evening, Mr Martyn," he said, trying to hide his surprise. "How may I be of service?"

Martyn's eyes darted past Jacob to the open door of the workshop behind him. Jacob stepped aside to allow him to enter, but Martyn shook his head. He thrust his hand into his coat pocket and came out with the watch Jacob had repaired.

"Take this, Silver," he said in a hoarse whisper. "Keep it safe."

"Certainly, sir, if you wish," Jacob said, taking it from him. "But can you tell me why?"

"Hide it. Don't tell anyone you have it. I may be wrong, and if I am, then I will return and retrieve it. But if I am not ..."

"Wrong about what, sir?"

Martyn shook his head again. He was in a state of extreme agitation, Jacob observed, and the best response seemed to be to follow his instructions without asking too many questions.

"Very well; I will keep the watch safe until you call for it," he said, keeping his voice as calm as possible.

"Good. Good. Don't give it to anyone else. Not to *anyone*."

"No, I won't. Is there anything else I should know?"

"You will know what to do when the time comes. *If* it comes. Instructions will be sent. Thank you, Silver."

Jacob started to reply, but Martyn turned abruptly and in a matter of seconds had vanished into the wet shadows. Jacob slipped the watch into his own pocket and closed the door.

He turned to go back to the kitchen and nearly fell over Sarah, who was standing only a pace or two behind him in the dark hallway. He hadn't even heard her approach.

"Come," he said, and she followed him back into the warm, lit kitchen. He closed the door behind them and said, "I suppose you heard what was said, what Mr Martyn asked me to do."

Sarah nodded, her eyes bright with curiosity. "What did he mean about being wrong?"

"I have no idea. Nor do I have any idea about why he wants me to hide the watch."

"Reckon he thinks someone is going to steal it."

"But who? And why give it to me, of all people, for safekeeping?"

"Reckon that's 'cause he can blame you then if it goes missing."

With an effort, Jacob suppressed a groan. Sarah's idea was all too plausible, and of course, he was on record with the police as having lost the watch once before, even though it had been returned.

"You may be right," he said reluctantly. "I had better find a safe place for it."

Sarah started to speak, then stopped abruptly.

"What is it?" Jacob asked her.

"I was going to say I could keep it, 'cause no one would ever think a housemaid would have something that fine," she said. "Course that depends on who's looking for it."

"You mean they might think, once a thief, always a thief?"

He regretted the words almost as soon as he had uttered them. Sarah nodded without meeting his eyes.

"Yes, sir," she murmured.

Jacob thought it over. "Mr Martyn charged me with the responsibility," he said. "I can't ask you to take the risk. But I appreciate the offer."

Sarah nodded again. "What are you going to do with it?"

"If I don't tell you, then you can honestly claim innocence," Jacob said. "With luck, the disaster – or whatever it is – that Mr Martyn envisions won't happen, and he'll come back for his watch. In the meantime …"

"I won't breathe a word, Mr Silver," Sarah said. "I ain't … I'm *not* stupid."

"I didn't think for a minute you were. But you're quite right; we mustn't mention this to anyone."

Jacob spent the remainder of the evening puzzling over Martyn's odd request and his even odder manner. The man had seemed almost frantic, as if he felt legions of demons or assassins were just behind him. Jacob hadn't seen anyone besides Martyn in the dark street, which brought up another question. How had he arrived? Although it wasn't a long walk from Church Green to the poorer end of Corn Street, it wasn't one a prosperous factory owner would normally undertake on his own after dark. The streets of Witney weren't nearly as dangerous as those of London, but there were still various dishonest – and occasionally violent – people abroad. Jacob shook his head.

Sarah didn't offer any further opinions on their visitor, so he assumed she was as mystified as he was. Finally, she finished her sewing and stood up, waiting for his dismissal.

"Will there be anything else, sir?"

"No, Sarah; go on to bed. Good night."

"Good night, Mr Silver."

She disappeared up the narrow staircase and Jacob sighed. He wished he had never agreed to repair Martyn's watch in the first place, but it was not in his nature to turn down work, and after all, he was the only person in Witney who could undertake such intricate repairs. That was one of the main reasons he had come here in the first place, because his mentor in Oxford had suggested there would be steady work in the smaller market town a few miles away. He had been correct, but Jacob suspected it was also to avoid the competition that would have arisen had they both continued working in the same place.

So he had purchased his small house with help from the Oxford community, and relocated himself and Leah, his father's dire predictions ringing in his ears. His father's death a year later had enabled him to pay back those who had loaned him money, but the old man had so far been correct when he said Jacob would always be an outsider, never fully accepted in the market town.

He stood up and stretched. Martyn's odd request had put him in a difficult situation, and the last thing he wanted was for the watch to be stolen again. Martyn might even, for some unknown reason, deny ever giving to him for safekeeping. So after a moment's thought, he carried it upstairs with him, wrapped it in a stocking and placed it under his pillow. It was a bit lumpy, but as he drifted into a restless sleep, he decided it was a sacrifice that had to be made.

Jacob woke with a start the following morning, his hand shooting under the pillow to check that the watch was still there. The lump he could feel through the cloth was reassuring and he breathed more easily.

He could hear Sarah moving about in the kitchen, and the scent of freshly brewed tea drifted up the stairs. For a moment he could almost believe he had dreamed the odd events of the night before, if not for the watch's physical presence. He took it out and gazed at it.

It was a fine watch; there was no doubt about that. Not only did it have considerable monetary value, as much as some families might earn in a year, but to the Martyns it was an heirloom, a reminder of a family member who had fought heroically for England at Waterloo. At least, Jacob thought wryly, he assumed the original owner had been heroic.

He made his way downstairs, the watch hidden deep inside his jacket pocket.

"Morning, Mr Silver," Sarah said.

"Good morning, Sarah." He suddenly remembered her announcement of the previous evening. "And many happy returns of the day."

"Thank you, sir."

"I'll have a boiled egg this morning, please."

"Yes, Mr Silver." She poured him a cup of tea and placed the saucepan for the egg on the stove. "Mrs Tucker brought some fresh eggs from her hens yesterday; I'll boil one of those."

Jacob nodded absently. His hand stole to his pocket, reassuring himself the watch was still safe. Sarah bustled around the kitchen and after a few minutes, placed the egg in front of him. He sliced the top off with his knife and dug into the golden yolk.

When he had finished eating, he went into the workshop, while Sarah cleaned the kitchen. He took a carriage clock and turned it over, carefully removing the plate that shielded the workings. Before touching anything, he took his glass out to examine it carefully, and was still holding this when a loud knock sounded on the door.

Jacob's head jerked up, remembering Martyn's visit, and wondered if he had returned so soon for his watch. His hand went to his pocket again as Sarah's voice said, "I'll see who it is, sir, shall I?"

Since this was properly a servant's job, Jacob let her go, but he laid the glass down and moved into the hallway behind her in case the situation required his presence.

Two men stood in the doorway, both of whom Jacob recognized. The first was the constable he had spoken to concerning the watch, and the other was Nathaniel Martyn.

"That's him, the thief," Nathaniel said. He pushed past Sarah and confronted Jacob, who felt a cold trickle of apprehension and took an instinctive step backward. Sarah hurried back into the kitchen while Jacob braced himself for whatever was coming.

"Good morning, Mr Martyn," he said, trying to keep his voice level. "Good morning, Constable."

"Search him," Nathaniel said, not bothering to acknowledge the greeting. "And then you can arrest him."

Jacob's heart sank. It appeared Sarah's prediction had been correct – he was going to be accused of stealing something valuable whose owner had entrusted it to him.

As he searched for words to explain the situation, the constable stepped forward.

"I shall have to ask you to empty your pockets, Mr Silver, if you please," he said.

Jacob sighed and began removing objects from his pockets. A handkerchief, a small pen knife, a bit of string, a few small coins. He placed them on the hall table and felt again in the depths of his pocket, wondering how he could possibly explain having the watch.

But his fingers encountered only the seams of the cloth. The watch wasn't there.

FIVE

Jacob fought to keep his face from reflecting his bewilderment. He turned both his jacket and trouser pockets inside out for the constable's inspection, revealing only a few bits of lint. He knew the watch had been in his jacket when he was eating his breakfast egg, and he also knew he hadn't dropped or removed it. But there was no time to worry about that now, not when Nathaniel's expression clearly showed both anger and frustration.

"Where is it?"

"What are you looking for, sir?" He tucked the linings back into place.

"My grandfather's gold watch. I know you have it. You stole it."

Jacob regained a portion of self-control. "If you recall, Mr Martyn, you were present when I returned it to your father."

The constable turned to Nathaniel. "Is that true, sir?"

Nathaniel didn't respond, but the sullen look on his face was answer enough.

"You are welcome to search my workshop, if you wish," Jacob added.

"I don't think that will be necessary," the constable said. "It would seem you are mistaken, Mr Martyn."

Nathaniel shot a look of pure hatred at Jacob, who wondered what he had done to deserve it. He had never seen the man before his call at the family home, and although he had formulated an instant, unflattering opinion, he had nothing definite to base it upon except Nathaniel's appalling manners and his father's assessment of him.

"Very well," Nathaniel said. He turned and stamped off. The constable nodded politely to Jacob and followed.

Jacob closed the door and exhaled in relief. Then he went into the kitchen, where Sarah was scrubbing the table vigorously.

"Where is it?" he asked her.

He was pleased to see that she didn't even pretend not to understand the question. She patted her skirt and said simply, "It's safe."

"Thank you. When did you take it?"

"When I saw who was at the door. You went past me to talk to them, remember?"

Jacob thought back and marveled that he hadn't been aware at all that she had even brushed against him, much less that she'd abstracted something from his pocket. No wonder she had been so successful at petty thievery – her small, nimble fingers were perfect for the job, as much tools of the trade as his own probes and calipers were for delicate repairs.

"And how did you know where I had put it?"

Sarah smiled. "You kept touching your pocket when you was eatin' breakfast, like you was checking something, so I reckoned that's where it was."

"It seems I must be more circumspect in future," he said.

"More what, sir?"

"Careful. Discreet. But we may have a more serious problem on our hands. I doubt that Mr Martyn confided in his son and in fact, may be trying to keep him from getting his hands on the watch. And yet, Nathaniel Martyn knew to come here searching for it. If I am going to be dragged into a family feud, I would like to know the reason."

"Maybe 'cause he knows you're honest?"

Jacob was touched by the compliment, but it didn't improve his outlook.

"I'm only a craftsman, not a relative or friend, or even an acquaintance."

Sarah wrung out the cloth she was using and turned to face him.

"Sometimes it's good to know people who ain't like you," she said.

"That may well be true. However, I think I shall call on Mr Martyn – the father, that is – this morning and see if he will tell me what this is all about."

Sarah said seriously, "Do you want me to come with you?"

"In what capacity? I admit you were extremely helpful this morning, but I hardly think Mr Martyn will welcome you into his house."

"Didn't think he would. I just thought someone might know something. So whilst you were talkin' to him, I could just ask around."

Jacob regarded her. "Don't you have work to do here?"

"Yes, sir." Sarah's face fell. "I'm helping Mrs Tucker with the washing."

"Good. You carry on with that. Don't worry, I shall keep you informed of any developments."

"Ta, Mr Silver."

Jacob clapped his rather battered felt hat on his head and put his coat on. He waited.

"Sarah."

"Yes, sir?"

"The watch?"

"Oh, yes." She smiled. "I almost forgot. Just a minute, sir."

She darted into the scullery and he heard rustling noises which he didn't want to interpret. A moment later she came out with the gold watch in her hand, and passed it to Jacob, who tucked it into his pocket.

"Good luck, sir."

"Thank you."

He set off down Corn Street at a brisk pace. The day was cool but sunny, a pleasant day in early autumn. If Jacob hadn't been so preoccupied, he would have enjoyed the walk. As it was, his intention was to return the watch to its rightful owner as quickly as possible and make it clear he wanted nothing more to do with it. Whatever Martyn's motives were, he would have to find someone else to entrust with the family heirloom.

At Church Green, Jacob went around to the tradesmen's entrance of Martyn's house, hoping Nathaniel had not returned home yet or at least would not see him arrive. The pretty dark-haired maid who answered the door shook her head, however, when he asked to see Thomas Martyn.

"He's not at home," she said, and catching his skeptical look, she giggled and added, "Really, sir, he's not here at all. He went off to the factory."

"Very well; I shall try to see him there. Thank you."

"Reckon that's not a good idea, sir. He was in a rare temper this morning."

Jacob paused, frowning. "Was he? I wonder why."

"Couldn't say, sir."

Jacob found himself wishing he had accepted Sarah's offer. She would know how to talk to the housemaid – might even be a friend of hers – and would probably have the entire story of Martyn's bad mood in a matter of minutes. He debated whether to pursue the subject and decided it would be better to locate Martyn and get his information from the horse's mouth, so to speak. So he gave the maid a warm smile, thanked her for her help and set off again in the autumn sunshine.

The blanket factory was a ten-minute walk away and Jacob was in no hurry. He spent the time rehearsing what he would say to Martyn, assuming he could get him on his own. It was hardly something he wanted others to hear about and judging by

48

Martyn's clandestine visit of the previous night, he, too, wanted it kept quiet. That could work in his favor.

Martyn's factory was one of several similar structures on the banks of the River Windrush, their peaked roofs and stacks visible from most of the town and even the surrounding fields. And that was fitting, since sheep from those fields and their by-products played such a large role in the lives of the local people – shepherds and shearers, fellmongers, tuckers, weavers, hauliers and factory workers, as well as those whose only connection was to sleep under wool blankets, wear wool coats and dine on mutton or lamb. Sheep even grazed on the elegant Church Green on occasion, reminding citizens of their importance to the local economy.

In particular, blankets made in Witney were famous around the world and the townspeople were justly proud of them. Jacob had walked past the factories many times, seeing workers going in and out or wagons being loaded in the yards to take the finished products to the new railway station.

He didn't have the faintest idea where in the Martyns' large factory he would be likely to find its owner, so he hovered in the street outside. Perhaps he shouldn't have come, but just kept the watch as Martyn had requested him to do.

Finally he steeled himself and walked through a door that appeared to be a main entrance. He expected to be challenged and he was, by a large burly man who blocked his path.

"Your business, sir?"

"I would like to speak briefly with Mr Thomas Martyn, if I may. My name is Jacob Silver."

"Oh, arr, I know who you are. The Jew."

Jacob smiled, trying to look more confident than he felt. "If you'd be kind enough to let him know I'm here? I won't take more than a few minutes of his time."

The man appeared to be debating whether to pick Jacob up bodily and throw him out – something he seemed quite capable of doing – or accede to his request. As he deliberated, a commotion came from the corridor behind them, a sound of angry voices and stamping footsteps.

Jacob recognized Martyn's voice as one of them and mentally gave the housemaid credit for accuracy. Martyn was indeed in a temper, and it was probably much worse now than it had been at his home, where he would attempt to control himself.

"There is no point in discussing this further," he was saying. "I've taken my decision."

"It is a very foolish decision, and one you will regret," said his companion. He was a tall, thin man whom Jacob vaguely remembered seeing in the town, but whose name he didn't know. Judging from his clothing and manner, he was well1 below Martyn on the social scale, which seemed to indicate their argument had to do with factory matters. His attitude as he faced up to Martyn, however, proved he had no intention of acknowledging the factory owner's superiority.

"I hope you don't intend that as a threat," Martyn said. "Collins here could break you into little pieces at my command." He indicated the large man who had stopped Jacob.

"Take it as you will. You have a responsibility to your employees, especially so in this case. And any violence will be met with violence."

Martyn stopped, seeing Jacob for the first time. He drew his eyebrows together. "Silver, why are you here?"

Something about the question told Jacob the honest answer wouldn't be the wise one. He had wanted to speak to Martyn on his own, and that clearly was not going to happen. Instead, he decided to steer a cautious path between the truth and purveying information.

"I had hoped to ask your opinion on a particular matter, sir," he said. "It has to do with your son. He came to my workshop this morning."

"Nathaniel?" Martyn was visibly startled, and the other man turned to stare at Jacob.

"Yes, sir. He seemed to think I had some … knowledge … on a particular subject and wished to consult me. I didn't think it would be of any use to him, so I declined. Do you think that was the correct course of action?"

He waited, hoping Martyn would be perceptive enough to understand what he was saying, that he had lied to Nathaniel about the watch's whereabouts.

"I believe you acted wisely," Martyn said, after a moment's thought. "Was Nathaniel content with that?"

"I think not."

"What are you blathering about?" asked the other man sharply, losing interest. "Martyn, you have one day to change your mind, and take the appropriate action. Whatever business you or your son have with this person is irrelevant."

Martyn turned back to face him. "And if I don't?"

"As I said, you will regret it."

"I doubt that. My decision is final. Good day."

For a brief moment, Jacob thought the argument was going to erupt into physical violence. Collins flexed his biceps in anticipation, but then the other man turned on his heel and strode out the door. Martyn glared at his retreating back.

"I apologize for that interruption, Silver," he said. "Mr Mead is under the mistaken impression that he can bully me into an unwise action."

Jacob had no idea what to say. "He seems rather strident," he observed.

"Oh, he is. Very strident. Represents the workers, he says. As if I didn't know what was best for them. All I ask of them – as my father did before me – is diligence, honesty and respectability."

Jacob had heard enough tales of factory life to question whether that was true, although rumor had it that Martyn's employees, despite their long hours, low pay and hard physical work, were actually treated better than those at some other mills and factories. At any rate, it was not an argument he wanted any part of. He wished the hulking bodyguard would leave, so he could speak to Martyn privately, but it appeared that wasn't going to happen.

"You remember what I told you, Silver," Martyn said. "I hope you have no intention of letting me down."

Jacob sighed. "No, sir, I shan't let you down," he said, and reluctantly turned to go.

He retraced his steps through the town, deep in thought. He hardly wanted to carry Martyn's watch around with him for the foreseeable future, so the next step was to find a place to conceal it safely. He wondered if he should consult Sarah on the matter; she possessed an insight into human nature he would never have. That might have been because of her semi-criminal activities or simply because she was female, but either way, he intended to take advantage of it.

By the time he returned to his house, he had formulated several theories concerning Martyn's actions, most of which he supposed were totally wrong. He hung up his hat and coat and went through the house to the scullery, where Sarah and Mrs Tucker were engaged in the lengthy business of doing the household laundry.

Sarah shot him a questioning look and he shook his head slightly. She smiled ruefully and turned back to the washing tub, sinking her arms up to the elbows in the hot soapy water.

Jacob left them to their work and went into his workshop. He removed Martyn's watch from his pocket and placed it in a drawer among other miscellaneous pieces of clock workings. It blended in fairly well, and he didn't think Nathaniel or the constable would bother to paw through the drawer, since they had already made one abortive foray. He still wondered how Nathaniel had known of his father's evening visit, but that was a problem for another day.

He locked the drawer and turned his attention to other jobs, and was so absorbed in those that it came as a surprise when Mrs Tucker put her head around the door and said, "I've left you a nice bowl of hot soup, Mr Silver, and the washing's all done, so I'm off home now."

"Thank you, Mrs Tucker," Jacob said. He laid down his tools and his glass and went into the kitchen. The soup, as promised, was hot, and thick with vegetables. He finished it off, his mind elsewhere, and then went in search of Sarah to consult her about a more permanent home for the watch.

She wasn't in the scullery, and a quick glance outside told him she wasn't hanging out washing in the garden, since it was already there, pegged up and flapping in the breeze. He listened, but didn't hear her footsteps overhead, so she wasn't upstairs, either. He frowned. It was possible she'd gone off to the market, but she rarely did that without telling him where she was going. One would expect, after all, to find a housemaid in the house.

He wasn't particularly worried, since Sarah could certainly look after herself, but it was still odd that she wasn't there. Just one more puzzling event in a strange day, he thought.

He returned to the workshop, wielding the delicate tools on an assortment of clocks and watches, trying not to look too often at the drawer which held Martyn's watch. It still stung that Sarah had so easily discovered the earlier hiding place.

The afternoon wore on and Sarah did not return. Jacob decided to look upstairs, on the off chance that she had been suddenly taken ill and was in her room, although surely Mrs Tucker would have mentioned it if that had been the case. He climbed the stairs and tapped lightly on the box room door. When there was no response, he pushed it open.

Sarah wasn't there, but the housemaid's dress and apron she had been wearing earlier hung neatly on a hook. Her other dress hung beside it. Jacob's eyebrows rose, but before he could draw a logical conclusion, he heard the scullery door below him open quietly and then close.

He retreated rapidly, closing the box room door and coming down the stairs at the same time that a breathless, somewhat scruffy urchin arrived in the kitchen. The patched pair of trousers, a ragged jacket and scuffed boots might have fooled most observers, but after a fortnight in the urchin's company, Jacob knew better.

"Where have you been, Sarah?" he asked sternly. "I hope you haven't been up to your old ways again."

"No, sir, not at all." Sarah pulled off the old wool cap that covered her hair, still much shorter than a girl's would be. Her face was grimy and she reached for the bowl of warm water on the back of the stove, splashing a handful to clean both her face and hands, then drying them on the linen towel. Jacob waited patiently.

"Then what have you been doing?" he asked when she put the towel down.

"Listening to people talk," Sarah said in surprise, as if there could be no other reason for her disguise. "Nobody takes notice of an errand boy hangin' around the Buttercross or the market square. And maybe asking a few questions in the right places."

"Lucky you didn't get your ears boxed for your impudence."

"I'm too quick for that, Mr Silver."

Jacob gave in to temptation. "All right, Sarah, did you learn anything of interest whilst you were eavesdropping and gossiping?"

Sarah settled herself on one of the chairs. In spite of the trousers, or perhaps because of them, she sat demurely, knees together and booted feet flat on the floor.

"I thought as maybe I'd get something out of the boot boy or the housemaid at Mr Martyn's house," she said. "Course I knew you'd been there this morning, and the housemaid – Gracie, her name is – said you'd gone off to find him at the factory. She thinks you're very handsome, by the way."

Jacob felt his face grow hot and hoped it didn't show. "Surely she didn't say that."

"She didn't have to. Anyway, seems like Mr Martyn's been in a temper for a week or more. No pleasin' him, and even his wife's starting to wonder what's wrong."

"I'm sure the housemaid didn't tell you that, either."

"Not in so many words, no. But take it as gospel." She shot him a glance. "Sorry."

Jacob smothered a smile. "Could it be because of some trouble at the factory? There's a man called Mead, who apparently claims to be representing the workers. He was threatening Mr Martyn when I was there."

"Oh, arr, he's a troublemaker, that one," Sarah said, nodding. "I knew some girls who worked there and thankful they were, too, to be getting steady wages. But Jerome Mead, he was always stirrin' people up, saying they should band together and stop work if they wasn't paid more."

"So is Mead a worker at the factory?"

"No, not exactly, but he's often there. He's a wool supplier, a middleman, you might say. He buys wool from them with sheep – the fleeces, you know, once they've been shorn – and sorts 'em and then sells the bales to the factory, so they can be scoured and blended and so on."

It occurred to Jacob that Sarah appeared to know far more about the process of how wool moved from sheep to finished blanket than he did. It was something he had never thought much about, and he resolved to educate himself, if only to prove his willingness to be part of a community that depended so heavily on the industry.

"I see. He seemed very sure of himself, as if he had some power to negotiate on behalf of the workers, but perhaps he's just a bombastic sort of person. I would think Mr Martyn – or whoever is responsible for purchasing the fleeces – could pick and choose where to buy his bales of wool. And they must buy from several sources, not just Mr Mead."

"Oh, I know they do, all them blankets and other things they make," Sarah agreed. "Must take a powerful lot of wool. But I reckon there's more to it than that."

"Oh?"

Sarah glanced around, as if expecting to find Mead lurking in a corner of the kitchen.

"Mead's been causin' trouble for a long time, but it's got worse of late. Gracie told me he actually came to Mr Martyn's house a few days ago, can you imagine?"

Under the circumstances, Jacob couldn't. A buyer and seller of fleeces who seemed intent on stirring up trouble at the blanket factory was an even more unlikely and unwelcome caller at the grand house than a Jewish watch repairer.

"I don't suppose the butler let him inside," he said.

"Oh, but he did," Sarah said. "As far as the scullery, that is. Then Mr Martyn came down himself to talk to him and they had a dreadful row. The servants heard 'em shouting at each other. It ended with Jerome Mead telling Mr Martyn if he didn't change his mind about somethin' – and nobody seems to know what – he'd kill him."

SIX

Jacob lifted his eyebrows.

"Do you suppose he meant it? If not, it would be a foolish thing to say, especially since it was obviously overheard."

"Dunno. Foolish thing to say, anyway, if he's talkin' about organizing the workers, 'cause if he *did* kill Mr Martyn, someone worse might take over."

It crossed Jacob's mind that the "someone" in question might well be Nathaniel, in which case Sarah's prediction would probably be all too accurate.

"That's very true. Did Mr Mead know his threat was overheard, I wonder?"

"Dunno that, either. I don't reckon he'd have servants, at least not proper ones, so he might not know how much they hear."

That was undeniably true. Jacob sat thinking for a moment, debating whether Mead's threats could have any bearing on Martyn's decision to visit after dark and leave a prized possession with Jacob for safekeeping. He didn't see how the two could be connected, but nothing about the matter seemed to make much sense. He decided to deal with a more immediate problem first.

"You'd better change into your own clothes," he said. "I don't suppose an errand boy would have thought about bringing anything back home to cook for supper?"

"Ah, you're wrong there, Mr Silver," Sarah said. She rummaged under her disreputable jacket and came out with an object he recognized as a thick slice of meat pie in a suet crust, wrapped in butcher's paper. "Venison, this is, being as I knew you wouldn't want pork pie. I'll do some carrots and cabbage to go with it."

"Did you steal that?"

"Course not," Sarah said. "I helped move some crates and things, and the butcher, he gave me this pie as payment."

Jacob wasn't entirely sure he believed her, but he was hungry enough to accept the explanation.

"Very well. Now go change back into being Sarah."

"Yes, sir."

She grinned at him and started for the stairs. Jacob watched her go and suddenly a thought occurred to him.

"By the way, does your imaginary young man have a name?"

"He's called Fred," she said promptly.

"You do realize," Jacob said, feeling a little embarrassed, "you will have to retire Fred before long? Once your hair grows out and you ..."

"Oh, arr," she said. "I know that. But he'll be useful for a bit longer."

Several hours later, Jacob lay in bed, staring at the dark ceiling. The venison pie had been delicious and he was glad Sarah had come to no harm during her masquerade, but he found it hard to sleep with all the questions crowding into his mind. Top of the list, of course, was why Martyn had left the watch with him a second time, but he also wondered what Nathaniel had planned and why Jerome Mead was threatening Martyn. It was hard to believe either Mead or Martyn could be so incensed over factory conditions, so perhaps there was some hidden agenda, some more personal link between the two men.

As he lay awake, he realized the wind was getting up; he could hear it howling and the branches of the apple tree in his garden scraping against the window pane. The small house almost seem to shake as some of the stronger gusts hit it. A proper autumn windstorm, he thought, one which would dislodge any loose roof slates and bring down weak branches. A driving rain, too, from the sound of it.

He eventually drifted off to sleep, tossing restlessly, and dreaming of gold watches that turned into handfuls of wool when he touched them.

He woke in the morning to find his prediction of foul weather had been fulfilled. Looking out of the bedroom window, he could see several branches had been ripped from their trees and lay along Corn Street. An autumn windstorm always did more damage than a winter one, since the leaves still on the trees gave the wind more of a grip. It wasn't unusual to see fallen branches, as there were today, and even an occasional toppled tree.

The road was wet from the rain, too, and promised to cake mud on the boots of anyone foolish enough to walk on it. Jacob did a quick mental survey of his current repair jobs to see if he needed to leave the house for anything and decided he didn't, at least not until it was a bit drier.

He went downstairs and found Sarah brewing the morning tea, which at least added an air of normality to the day. Perhaps it wouldn't be as bad as he had feared.

"Morning, Mr Silver," she said cheerfully. "Blew a gale last night, didn't it?"

"It certainly did. There seem to be quite a few branches down."

"I'll pour a cup of tea and have your breakfast for you in a minute, sir."

"There's no hurry." Jacob accepted the cup of hot tea and sat at the table.

Sarah moved around the kitchen, eventually depositing a plate containing a sizzling kipper and a thick slice of bread and butter in front of him. He assumed she had already eaten, as she made no move to serve herself anything beyond a cup of tea.

"I'll go to the market this morning and get some more carrots and parsnips, maybe an onion as well," she said, sipping the tea.

"Take care on the road if you do," Jacob said. "It's very muddy at the moment and easy to slip. For myself, I'm hoping it will dry a bit before I need to go out."

"Ah, well, you've got finer boots than me, Mr Silver. Be a shame to muddy them up."

Jacob glanced at her and caught a twinkle in the blue eyes watching him over the rim of the teacup. He decided she was teasing him, something decidedly unacceptable from a housemaid, but somehow inoffensive coming from Sarah.

"Very well, but don't say I didn't warn you."

"No, sir." Sarah removed his empty plate and took it to the scullery for washing. She returned to the kitchen carrying her woolen shawl and the marketing basket. "I shan't be long."

Jacob watched her go, standing at the door until she disappeared from sight over the crest of the gentle hill that rose between his house and the main crossroads of the town. He wasn't quite sure what he would have done if she had slipped and fallen in the mud, but he felt responsible for her welfare. He shook his head, knowing he wouldn't have had the same concern about Mrs Tucker – not that he would be able to lift her if she fell – and went back into his workshop.

He had been working for perhaps an hour when he felt the familiar anxiety. Why hadn't Sarah come back from the market? Even with the mud to consider, it shouldn't have taken her long to purchase a few vegetables and perhaps a piece of fish for the evening meal.

He went to the door and looked up the road. A wave of relief washed over him as he saw Sarah at the top of the hill, which changed to surprise as he realized she was hurrying, almost running, her boots sliding on the slippery surface. She reached his gate and grasped the post to steady herself, as Jacob held the door open.

Sarah slipped inside and leaned against the door, panting.

"What on earth's the matter?" Jacob asked her.

She didn't answer immediately, but set the basket on the floor and then bent down to pull off her boots. As predicted, they were very muddy, and she clutched them in one hand so as not to track mud across the floor.

"It's that Mr Martyn, sir," she said, still slightly breathless.

"What about him?"

"He's dead, sir. Stone cold dead."

Jacob felt an icy shiver of dread go down his spine.

"How do you know that?"

"Bless you, sir, everyone was talking about it. And I saw him, as well."

Jacob took a deep breath and said, "Come into the kitchen, Sarah, and tell me what happened."

Sarah hung up her shawl and propped her wet boots against the stove to dry while Jacob waited. They sat down on either side of the pine table.

She said, "I was just coming up to the Buttercross and I saw a whole crowd of people on the far side of Church Green where Mr Martyn's house is. The constables were there and all, and that Dr Sheridan what lives opposite Market Square."

Jacob nodded. He was familiar with Sheridan, who had battled to save Leah and Miriam. He was a competent doctor and had even refused an offer of payment after their deaths, saying he had done everything he could but had failed, so didn't expect Jacob to pay him. It had been an unexpectedly generous gesture and Jacob still felt himself in the doctor's debt.

"So of course I had to go see what they was all looking at," Sarah continued.

"Of course."

"Some branches come down off one of those big trees along the side of Church Green. Great big ones, and one of them must have hit him. Crushed him, like."

"But why would he …"

"I know, sir. Why was he outdoors at night in a storm like that? Terrible windy, it was, and raining as well."

"Exactly."

"'Cause the wind didn't get up until late. At least ten or eleven, maybe later. So it'd have been after that."

Jacob nodded. It seemed Thomas Martyn had made a habit of after-dark outings, with no obvious explanation for them. Several theories flitted through his mind, and as usual, Sarah was one step ahead of him.

"Unless he was meeting somebody," she said.

"It would have had to be an important meeting, so drag him out in weather like that," he said. He wasn't sure how aware Sarah would be of another reason a man might be out on his own after dark, but she nodded seriously.

"Girls working the street wouldn't be out in a storm like that," she said, as Jacob mentally pictured prostitutes seeking shelter from the wind and rain under the sturdy slate roof of the Buttercross. "Not for long, anyway. Maybe he was meeting Jerome Mead, do you think?"

"Possibly. Or someone else. But why so secretively?"

"Dunno."

Jacob drummed his fingertips on the table. "You said you actually saw Mr Martyn, Sarah. And a branch had fallen on him?"

"Oh, arr, a big one." She held up her hands about four inches apart to indicate the diameter. "Right across his chest, it was. Reckon it smashed him, broke his ribs. There was lots of little branches coming out from it and leaves, too, half a tree almost, but I could see his boots sticking out."

Jacob imagined the scene and winced, not just at the fatal event itself but at the curious onlookers who would have seen it as a sort of gruesome entertainment. That unfortunately included Sarah, who seemed unmoved by Martyn's fate. Perhaps she considered it repayment or divine retribution for his treatment of her mother. He wrenched his mind back to the cold hard facts.

"But someone must have pulled the branches off, at least enough for the doctor to be able to examine him."

"The constables were trying to, I think. They was telling everyone to stand back, but of course they didn't. And anyway, there weren't nothing the doctor could do. He said so. Mr Martyn was already dead, maybe for hours before anyone knew."

Jacob sighed. The violent death of a leading figure in the town would naturally be of interest to anyone in the vicinity, and the news would spread rapidly. It was too much to expect of human nature for the crowds to obediently melt away on the constables' orders and ignore the drama.

"I wonder who first found him," he said.

"Think it was the baker's boy," Sarah said. "He was still there, white as a sheet, telling everybody as how he'd been pushing his cart along real early in the morning, and cursin' 'cause the branches that fell down were getting in his way, and then he saw these big branches fallen down with somebody under 'em. So he ran across Church Green to the police station and fetched the constable and the sergeant."

"And they must have sent for the doctor. Did Dr Sheridan say anything?"

"Not that I heard. Except that he was dead and the family should be told."

"But wouldn't they already know?" Jacob asked in surprise. "It sounds like he died more or less on his own doorstep and surely they would have noticed he wasn't in the house."

Sarah shook her head. "You'd think not, sir, but my ma told me rich people don't live like us. His wife, she might have been sleeping in her own bedroom and having breakfast by herself there. Her maid would have brought it up, so she wouldn't see her husband first thing, and she'd maybe have thought he was up early and gone to the factory or somewhere."

That was possible, Jacob thought, amused that Sarah had lumped herself in with him on the social scale. Mrs Martyn might well not have realized her husband wasn't at home, and who knew what communication there normally was between Nathaniel and his father. If servants had noticed the master of the house was missing, they probably wouldn't have thought it their place to draw attention to the fact.

"And what happened after Dr Sheridan had been? Was the undertaker summoned?"

"Expect so, sir, but I didn't stop there. I thought you should know, so I came back here."

The cold shiver went down Jacob's spine again. Being in possession of a gold watch belonging to a man who had died suddenly and dramatically was not a good position to be in. There was no one but Sarah to back up his claim that Martyn had asked him to keep – hide – the watch, and given her reputation with the local police, it was unlikely they'd believe her. No wonder she had hurried back to give him the news, not that either of them had much in the way of defenses to rally.

She watched him, following his thoughts. "Not much we can do about it, is there, Mr Silver?"

"Not at the moment, no. So I think the best thing is to go about our work as if nothing has happened."

"What if Mrs Tucker comes in full of the news?"

Jacob hadn't considered that.

"You may have been seen in Church Green, Sarah, so the best thing would be to tell the truth. You were on your way to the market and saw a crowd of people, so you were curious and went to see what they were looking at."

"Do I know anything else?"

"I shouldn't think so. No one tells a housemaid all the details of a tragic death, do they? Or the events leading up to it, if that becomes relevant."

Their eyes met and Sarah smiled.

"I'll go back to the market this afternoon and see if there's anything else been learned. Reckon nothing this interesting's happened here for a long time, so people will be talking about it."

"If you wish, but please, not as Fred. I admit he may be useful on some occasions, but this isn't one of them. Go as yourself, displaying a modest but natural curiosity."

"Oh, arr, I can do that. Besides, with all the excitement, I never got them carrots and parsnips, so I'd have to go back to the greengrocer's."

"I see. And I shall be going into town myself this morning. I have a clock to return to its owner."

"Would he live in Church Green, sir?" Sarah asked innocently.

"No, but just off it, near the brewery. John Rexford, the solicitor."

She nodded. "So you could learn something, maybe, 'cause Mrs Rexford's maid says she's a dreadful gossip."

"Yes, I've met Mrs Rexford. She's quite … chatty. But Sarah, no one must know about that watch that Mr Martyn left it here."

"Course not. Mr Silver?"

"Yes?"

"You remember when he was here, Mr Martyn said he might be wrong about something?"

Jacob thought back to Martyn's furtive night time visit and the man's unusual manner.

"Yes, I do."

"Looks to me like he may have been right."

SEVEN

Jacob couldn't really argue with that statement, even though he still had no idea what Martyn had been referring to. However, his immediate concern was that neither he nor Sarah be blamed for – or even associated with – the man's unfortunate death.

Sarah stood up and went to put the empty basket back into the scullery. When she returned, she said, "Mr Silver?"

"Yes?"

"You reckon a big, heavy branch just happened to fall off that tree and hit Mr Martyn in the right place to kill him?"

Jacob had to admit he'd been thinking much the same thing.

"I don't know, Sarah, but I don't think we should speculate about it, at least not openly."

"What's 'speculate' mean, sir?"

"It means guessing what may have happened. We'll find out soon enough, I imagine. And it is possible that he was just very unfortunate."

She gave him a scornful glance. "I don't believe that and you don't either, I can tell."

"Possibly not, but I like the alternative even less."

"You mean that someone on purpose …"

"Ssh," Jacob said hastily. He had heard Mrs Tucker approaching across the garden, her feet squelching through the wet grass.

Sarah bent down and retrieved her boots, slipping her feet into them and buttoning the tops.

"Wonder what she'll say," she murmured.

"You can tell me later." Jacob was in no mood to listen to Mrs Tucker's recital of the morning's events, assuming she had passed that way and picked up the gossip. He went into his workshop and pointedly closed the door behind him.

He could hear Mrs Tucker's voice, excitedly relaying the news, and Sarah politely asking questions and inserting comments. He doubted that Mrs Tucker knew anything he and Sarah didn't, but it was always possible, so he didn't interrupt their conversation, knowing Sarah would pass on anything of interest.

Eventually their voices faded as they went upstairs to clean the bedrooms, and Jacob bent over his work with renewed concentration. He replaced the clasp on a string of pearls and cleaned a ring so the gems set in it were displayed in all their glory. Then he put the jewelry safely away in a locked drawer, trying hard not to glance at the one below it holding Martyn's watch. He picked up the clock he was delivering and placed it in a cloth bag, collected his coat and hat and went out the door.

Corn Street had dried out enough by this time that he had no trouble walking between his house and the Buttercross. He stopped there for a moment, noting that the site of Martyn's demise was still drawing attention, perhaps because the large branch that had crushed him had not yet been removed. Jacob could see several young boys darting around it and snipping smaller twigs off, which they would no doubt be keeping, or even selling, as grisly souvenirs.

The branch had probably been shifted to allow the removal of Martyn's body, but it couldn't have been moved far because of its size. Sarah hadn't exaggerated by much when she described it as half a tree, although a strong or determined man, Jacob estimated, could have dragged it a short distance. That meant Thomas Martyn had died within a few yards of his own front door, but whether he had been leaving the house, returning to it or merely stepping outside for a moment was unclear.

A butler came out of the house and chased the boys off, and judging by the exasperated expression on his face, not for the first time. Jacob noted that the house windows were already draped in black, and straw had been laid on the gravel path in front to muffle the sound of passing carts and carriages.

The butler and the rest of the staff would have their work cut out for them, he reflected, considering that they would have to deal not only with a grieving family but a morbidly curious public. Violent death might be fairly common in a large city like London, but not in a small Cotswold market town.

Aside from the Duke of Marlborough, residing in splendor at Blenheim Palace a few miles away, members of the aristocracy were thin on the ground here. That meant wealthy men such as Martyn, who might have been snubbed in London for their trade associations, were accorded a certain status. And one who had managed to die in such a spectacular fashion could expect to draw even more attention. Martyn's funeral, Jacob predicted, would be one of the social highlights of the year.

Jacob, on the other hand, had learned to melt into the background when possible, so he resolutely turned his back on the Martyn residence and started down the opposite side of the green. Halfway down, he turned into a short cul-de-sac, and approached a substantial stone house, not quite as grand as the Martyns', but both elegant and solid. As usual, he went to the tradesmen's entrance and waited to be seen.

He expected a warmer welcome than the one he had received at the Martyn residence and this proved to be the case. The owner of the house was a successful solicitor and his previous brief encounter with Jacob had been courteous, but businesslike. The solicitor's wife, however, had taken pity on him because she knew of his bereavement, clucked over him like a plump, friendly hen and offered him a cup of tea and a slice of cake in the parlor, no less, chatting all the while.

Jacob had been amazed and somewhat touched by her concern, wondering if she imagined he had been living on bread and water since Leah's death, but he had been happy to accept her hospitality. It was rare enough for him to be tolerated in the town's finer houses, let alone welcomed and fed.

This time she bustled into the entry way, beaming at him as if at an old friend.

"Good morning, Mr Silver. My husband said you might come by today. You've brought the clock back?"

"Good morning, Mrs Rexford. Yes, I've repaired it and it's working well now."

He took it from the bag and handed it to her. She turned it around and looked at it admiringly.

"I'm so pleased. It usually lives in the parlor and we've missed it, I must say. One doesn't really notice something like a clock until it isn't there any more, or isn't telling the correct time."

"Yes, I know what you mean," Jacob said. "It's very frustrating."

"Although I don't imagine you ever have the same problem, being so good at repairing things. Thank you for returning it so quickly. Now, cook's just made some scones; would you like one with a cup of tea?"

"Thank you, yes, if it's no trouble."

"Of course not." She turned to a hovering housemaid, who was surveying Jacob with frank curiosity while pretending not to do so. "Millie, scones and tea for two in the parlor, please. This way, Mr Silver."

Jacob followed her into the cozy room where a coal fire provided welcome warmth against the autumn chill. He reflected that she must be very confident of her place in the social hierarchy to risk sharing tea and scones on her own with an unmarried man, and the town heretic as well. It was an action, however kindly meant, that would have earned social condemnation for most women, and Mrs Rexford was too conventional to be deliberately inviting scandal by flouting the social code.

For his own part, he suspected she might have some additional information on the Martyns – dead and alive – and although he felt slightly guilty about trying to extract it, he decided the ends justified the means. Not that he would have to try very hard, given his hostess's talkative nature.

His last shreds of guilt disappeared when the maid arrived with a tray bearing the scones and tea. The scones were light and fluffy, served with butter and strawberry preserves, and the tea hot and fragrant. Mrs Rexford poured him a cup, continuing with the monologue she had started as soon as they were seated.

"So of course hearing all that commotion across the green, Alfred – our boot boy, you know – went out to see what was going on, and he found it was because of Thomas Martyn being caught by a falling branch during that terrible storm last night and crushed to death, poor man. Sugar, Mr Silver?"

"No, thank you," Jacob said.

"Such a pity, and such a dreadful way to die. I do hope it was quick and that he didn't suffer for long. It really does make one believe God moves in mysterious ways." She glanced up quickly. "Oh, perhaps I shouldn't have said that. I didn't mean to offend you."

Jacob smiled. "I, too, believe in God."

"Oh, yes, I suppose you do. Yes, of course."

He could see her rapidly trying to extricate herself from a theological discussion. To help her out, he said, "I'm sure Mr Martyn's family will be greatly distressed. Any death is upsetting, but such a sudden, unexpected death must be even worse for them."

"Yes, poor Evangeline. His wife, you know. A lovely woman."

Mrs Rexford sipped her tea, her genuine sympathy obviously tinged with a certain amount of ghoulish enjoyment. Jacob couldn't really blame her, since her normal daily activities would encompass running the household, social calls, perhaps a bit of charitable work and not much else. He expected that poor Evangeline would be swamped with visitors before long, all of them offering condolences and looking for gossip.

"I've not had the pleasure of meeting Mrs Martyn," Jacob said. "However, I have met Nathaniel, her son. Do you suppose he will be taking over the running of the factory after his father's death?"

"I couldn't say," Mrs Rexford said, suddenly cautious. Jacob cursed himself for pushing the conversation too far, too fast.

"Or perhaps there are other relatives who will be involved," he said, trying to keep his tone casual.

"Perhaps. I believe there's a nephew – no, two – in Birmingham, his sister's sons."

She made Birmingham, eighty miles to the north, sound like the ends of the earth. Jacob nodded and she continued.

"I've always thought it was such a shame that Frederick, his elder son, died of typhoid. A very pleasant young man, he was, nothing like …"

She cut off her words, but Jacob, having met Frederick's brother, had no difficulty imagining how the sentence would have ended.

"Ah, well, I'm sure it will all work out," he said. He took a bite of his scone and washed it down with a mouthful of tea.

"I'm sure it will," Mrs Rexford agreed. "I would think Thomas Martyn had made provisions in his will for the future of the factory, so it will all be handled in a legal, straightforward manner. Not that I know anything about it."

Jacob hadn't thought of that, but it was something to consider. He started to ask a question, stopped, and was glad he had when Mrs Rexford added, "He was a client of my husband's, you see. In fact, he was here speaking to John in his office just a day or two ago, almost as if he had had a premonition."

"I see." He was amused that she was claiming total ignorance of legal matters – an appropriate stance for a wife – when she probably was as aware as her husband of the provisions of Thomas Martyn's will. Martyn's recent visit might have concerned his will, or it might have been because of an entirely different subject. Still, there was no point in pursuing it, since even Mrs Rexford's volubility had its limits. It would be a confidential legal matter, so she wouldn't tell him even if she knew, and it was unlikely to affect him personally.

He asked casually, "Are there children other than Nathaniel? He is the only one I am aware of."

"Yes, there is a daughter, Charlotte. She is married to a doctor and lives in Oxford. I believe she has a child, perhaps two."

Jacob nodded politely. The unspoken subtext was that Charlotte might benefit financially from her father's death, but she was being amply provided for by her husband and anything she inherited would become his property anyway. Jacob dismissed Charlotte, as least temporarily, from his thoughts.

"More tea, Mr Silver?"

"No thank you, Mrs Rexford. It was delicious, but I must be getting back to my workshop."

"Of course. I hope I didn't detain you unnecessarily."

Jacob smiled. "Not at all. And it was well worth it, both for the refreshment and the company. Thank you again."

He let Mrs Rexford see him out, noting that she might be willing to entertain him, but was still prudent enough to make him leave the house through the tradesmen's entrance, his final departure overseen by the maid. He chuckled to himself at the thought. He might have risen a little in his hostess's estimation, but not quite enough to be respectable.

Once back in Church Green, he debated whether to go straight home or see if any more snippets of information might be available. He looked across the grassy expanse and discovered that while he had been talking with Mrs Rexford, men had arrived to remove the lethal branch, which aside from anything else, was obstructing the pathway around the green. The drivers of delivery carts and carriages would not be amused at having to circumnavigate the entire green if their destination was just beyond the blocked portion.

Jacob decided that anyone might be justifiably curious about the men's work, so he stood for a while and watched. They had begun by cutting off the smaller branches, loading them into a cart for removal, and were now working their way toward the thick central branch which had landed on Thomas Martyn's chest.

He shifted his gaze upward to the tree from which the branch had fallen. A raw gash surrounded by splintered bits of wood marked the place where the branch had been attached to the trunk before the wind had ripped it loose. Had it after all just been an unfortunate accident? Jacob wanted to think so, but like Sarah, he found himself very skeptical, especially in the light of Jerome Mead's threats. But how could Mead, or anyone else, have counted on nature being so helpful in disposing of someone they wanted to injure or kill?

He was still pondering the likelihood of Thomas Martyn standing in the wrong place at the wrong time, and not moving when he heard the branch crack overhead, when a flurry of activity made him turn his head.

The door of the new police station had opened and three men came out, two of them in uniform. Jacob recognized one as the constable he had dealt with previously, and the second was a sergeant, the town's only other full-time police officer. Between them was Dr Sheridan, his face set in grim lines, and all three were striding purposefully across the green.

Jacob instantly knew something was seriously wrong. He remembered Sarah saying the doctor had been called out to see if there was anything he could do to save Martyn's life and when it became obvious he couldn't, his role in the drama would have ended. His presence at the police station, however, seemed to indicate there was more to the picture than it first appeared, and the fact that the officers were accompanying him to the fatal site only emphasized that.

The trio were heading his direction, which ordinarily would have been the cue for Jacob to melt unobtrusively away, since it had become second nature for him to avoid being noticed. But he knew Sarah would never forgive him if he didn't try to find out what was going on, so he simply took a few steps to move out of the path of the approaching men.

They were so intent on their mission that it seemed he was going to be completely ignored, which suited him, but at the last minute Dr Sheridan spotted him and said, "Good morning, Silver."

"Good morning, Doctor," Jacob replied.

He rather hoped the greeting would be all that was required of him, but Sheridan stopped short and stared at him, as if struck by an idea.

"Do you have your glass with you?" he asked abruptly.

"I beg your pardon?"

"The glass that you use for close work, for magnification," Sheridan clarified.

"Oh. No, I'm afraid not. It's in my workshop."

"Pity."

Jacob opened his mouth to ask why, and then decided he might not want to know. "I can fetch it if it's needed," he offered.

"No, no, that's all right. Would have been useful, but can't expect you to carry the tools of your trade around with you."

There seemed to be no answer to that, but since no one had asked him to leave, Jacob followed at a discreet distance as the three men turned their backs on him and neared the tree. All three bent over the large branch, examining it closely. Burning with curiosity, Jacob edged a little nearer. As far as he could see, they were looking at a particular section of the branch, and by squinting, he could see some darker reddish-brown marks on the smooth bark, possibly bloodstains. That was reasonable, he thought, considering the force with which it must have struck Martyn.

The doctor was now pointing to the stained bark and saying something in a low voice which Jacob couldn't quite catch. Both police officers nodded seriously, and the sergeant turned and spoke to the workmen who had been cutting the branches up, receiving what was clearly a negative response.

"In that case, they may as well remove the rest of it," Sheridan said, loudly enough for Jacob to hear. "It's only blocking the path and will yield no more information." He turned to the workmen. "However, I would like to retain that stained part of the branch. Cut it on either side, please, and bring that section to my surgery."

He and the police moved off, gesturing for the workmen to continue. Jacob stayed rooted to the spot, watching the men laboriously sawing the branch into sections small enough to move. Finally he decided there was nothing more to be seen or learned, and turned to go. As he did, however, Sheridan and the officers moved back in his direction, and he could catch snatches of their conversation.

The words "inspector", "higher authority" and "suspicion" floated back to him, all seeming to indicate that Thomas Martyn's death might not have simply been the result of being hit by a random falling branch during a windstorm. It sounded as though a joint decision had been made that someone more experienced than the local constables should establish exactly what had happened.

And that became even clearer a minute later when the three men moved toward the Martyn house and Jacob heard Sheridan say, "I know it will be a shock to the family, Sergeant Bell, but I believe we have to consider the distinct possibility that this was *not* an accident."

EIGHT

Jacob found he wasn't too surprised by Sheridan's statement, and it the police officers didn't seem to be, either. All three men darted a glance in his direction, but all they saw was his retreating back, since Jacob had turned and was starting across the green on his way home. He would have liked to stay and see if he could gauge the family's reaction, but he doubted he would be allowed close enough, and how on earth could he justify his curiosity? The only excuse would be to reveal his stewardship of the gold watch, something he had no intention of doing.

So he walked briskly back down Corn Street until he reached his own house. He put a hand into his pocket for the key, but Sarah opened the door before he could take it out. From the expression on her face, he assumed Mrs Tucker had gone home and she was eager for an update.

"Did you hear anything, sir?" she asked, even before he could hang up his coat and hat.

"Yes, I did. Most of it you already know."

"Oh." Sarah's disappointment was clear.

"And one thing you aren't aware of."

Her face brightened instantly. "Yes?"

"Dr Sheridan thinks Mr Martyn's death was not an accident. And he's told the family so. Or at least I believe he has. He and the police were at Martyn's door when I left to come here."

"So the doctor thinks somebody did him in," Sarah said thoughtfully. "Murdered him. What makes him think so?"

"I don't know. Something to do with the bark on the tree branch, I believe."

Sarah's blue eyes grew wide. "The bark? What could that be?"

"I've no idea. There seemed to be some bloodstains on it, but that's to be expected, I would think."

Jacob sat down at the table and after a moment's hesitation, Sarah sat opposite him. She appeared to be thinking deeply.

"My little brother, he dropped a stone on his foot once. It went all red and purple and I think one of the bones got broke, but there weren't no blood."

"Because the skin wasn't broken, only badly bruised, I suppose," Jacob said. "But this wasn't a stone; it was a large, heavy branch falling from a great height. I didn't see Martyn's body, but still …"

"So if the doctor thinks he was killed and it wasn't an accident, then he must have seen something else."

"Yes. He must have done."

Jacob pondered in silence until Sarah finally said, "You look ever so serious, Mr Silver. You want something to eat, maybe?"

"Only a bit. Mrs Rexford gave me tea and scones."

"Ooh." Sarah made a face. "You're moving up in society, ain't you?"

"Sarah."

"*Aren't* you moving, up, I mean."

"Hardly. She simply wanted someone to gossip with, and I was available."

Jacob felt that somewhere along the way he had lost some of his authority over Sarah, who was regarding him with amusement. And the odd thing was that he didn't mind her gentle teasing, even in the current uncertain situation. She might

77

be unpredictable in some ways, but he felt her loyalty to him was sincere and unquestionable.

"Expect she wanted to show how daring she was, having tea with someone like you," she said, her mouth twitching into a smile. "But never mind. I'll get you some soup."

She moved to the stove, where the ever-present pan of soup simmered. As she dished it up, she added, "It's good and hot, but it may not agree with you and then you'd have to call the doctor out, wouldn't you?"

Much as he wanted to speak to Sheridan on his own, Jacob felt obliged to object to this helpful suggestion.

"I think that's a bit too obvious, Sarah. After all, he saw me on Church Green not half an hour ago and even spoke to me. If I claimed a sudden illness he'd know I was lying."

"Could be I'd have something wrong with me, then. Trouble is, it'd have to be serious to get the doctor out for a housemaid."

"True. On the other hand, we could simply mind our own business and let the local police or whoever is called in to assist them discover the truth."

Sarah just looked at him. "With that watch still in your workshop, Mr Silver? That Mr Nathaniel will be back looking for it, mark my words, and a locked drawer won't stop him."

Jacob stopped himself from groaning audibly. She was right, of course, as she usually was.

"Let's have the soup first," he said. "We may think of something afterwards."

"Mr Silver?"

"Yes, Sarah?"

"Glad to hear it's 'we' and not just you."

Jacob finished his soup, but a minute later couldn't recall what the ingredients had been. In an effort to concentrate his mind, he thanked Sarah for the meal and went into his workshop. He sat on the stool and stared at the locked drawer where Martyn's watch lay, resisting the temptation to take it out and … what?

Drop it in the River Windrush and pretend he knew nothing about it? No, that wouldn't do. *I'm too honest*, he told himself, *and at the moment, that's a disadvantage. And besides, it's a fine watch, far too good to throw away.*

He heard the scullery door close and knew Sarah – or possibly Fred, despite his admonition – had gone into town to glean any more available information. He found himself hoping that Sheridan had been mistaken, but the man was too competent a doctor for that.

He turned his attention to a pocket watch he was cleaning, wishing it didn't remind him of Martyn. Jacob hadn't particularly liked the man, but he hadn't wished him ill, either. Someone had done, however, or Martyn would still be alive.

The obvious suspect was Jerome Mead, who had a history of conflict with Martyn and who had publicly threatened him. Jacob couldn't help feeling that had been an imprudent action, since quite a few people knew of the antagonism between them.

But who else? Jacob knew there might be a long list of disgruntled factory workers, suppliers of fleeces, hauliers and other business-related contacts who might not be immediately obvious. Martyn might have contracted personal debts he hadn't paid, cheated at cards or failed to pay a prostitute, all of which would have brought violent retribution. On the other hand, would any of those potential enemies have been lurking outside his house during a wind storm, and then taking advantage of nature's fury to dispose of him? It seemed unlikely.

He supposed that in a way, Sarah could be added to the list, considering Martyn's indifference to her mother's plight and Sarah's reaction to it. There might be other unhappy household staff, present or past, who had suffered at his hands. And had Sarah not returned the watch when she had, Jacob himself might have been among those happy to see Thomas Martyn crushed under half a tree.

It was rather depressing to realize how many people the man might have antagonized and Jacob was still considering this when someone knocked at the scullery door.

He got up and went to open the door. A boy of perhaps ten or eleven stood outside, his cap in his hand. His clothes were almost threadbare; he was grimy from head to foot, and he was breathing hard, as if he'd run a long way.

"You Mr Silver?"

"Yes."

"Doctor sent me to fetch you. Doctor Sheridan. Says you're to come to his surgery."

Jacob's eyebrows flew upward. His first thought was that Sarah had somehow fabricated an excuse to bring him and Sheridan together, although he hated to think what it could be. It was too much to expect the doctor to consult him for any other reason.

"Did he say why?"

The boy shrugged. He'd delivered his message, and after looking at Jacob's house, he knew he couldn't expect much in the way of a reward. The reasons behind the message didn't concern him.

"Somethin' 'bout a girl, he said. A maid."

So it *was* Sarah. Jacob felt in his pocket and handed the boy two pennies.

"Thank you. I'll come at once."

"Ta, mister."

The boy shot off through the garden and down the alley. Jacob closed the scullery door and collected his coat and hat. He paused, and then went into his workshop to get his magnifying glass before leaving via the front door. This time, it might be called into use.

He walked up Corn Street again to the Buttercross, but instead of turning right into Church Green as he had earlier in the day, he turned left into the High Street, which formed one side of Market Square. Sheridan's surgery faced the square and Jacob lifted the brass knocker on its front door, reasoning that since he had been summoned, he didn't need to seek the tradesman's entrance.

The door was opened by a woman whom Jacob assumed was either the doctor's housekeeper or possibly a nurse, one of the women who had learned her profession nursing soldiers in the Crimea. Either way, she exuded an air of competence and efficiency. She seemed unsurprised to see him and before he could identify himself, she said, "This way, Mr Silver."

Jacob followed her into a room which was clearly used for examining patients. Shelves held jars and medical equipment, and there was a raised, flat bed in the center, covered by a clean white sheet.

Sheridan was standing by a sink, washing his hands, and Sarah was sitting on one of the three hard-backed chairs. A white bandage was fastened snugly around her forehead, hiding most of her short hair, and even from across the room, Jacob could see that she looked shaken and much paler than normal. Any thought he had had of scolding her for faking an injury rapidly disappeared, to be replaced by concern.

"Ah, Silver," Sheridan said, turning. "I'm glad you are here." He gestured toward Sarah. "Miss Simm tells me she is in your employ."

"That's right, sir."

"Do her duties normally include theft?"

Jacob's mouth dropped open and he snapped it shut. He transferred his astonished gaze from the doctor to Sarah.

"No, they do not. What on earth have you been doing, Sarah?"

"Wasn't doing nothin', Mr Silver."

"So how did you come by that, doing nothing?" He indicated her bandage.

"Fell down and cut my head, sir."

Jacob turned to Sheridan. "I'm not questioning your statement, doctor, but what theft are you referring to?"

"The Martyn residence. As you are aware, Thomas Martyn died during the night and understandably, the household is in something of a turmoil. The girl sought to take advantage of this,

I'm told, by attempting to make off with some items from the kitchen. Silver spoons, I believe."

"Is that true, Sarah?"

"No, sir."

It was such a flat statement that both men looked at her in surprise. Jacob reviewed Sheridan's statement and said, "Doctor, you said you were told this. By whom?"

Sheridan frowned. "Nathaniel Martyn."

"Does he often visit the kitchen and count the cutlery, I wonder?"

Sheridan threw a shrewd glance at Jacob and then said slowly, "I see your point, Silver. However, that doesn't mean the information was incorrect. Were you in the kitchen of the Martyn residence, Miss Simm?"

"Only to pass a word or two with one of the kitchen maids I know, sir."

"Did you steal anything?"

"No, sir."

"How did you injure yourself?" Jacob asked.

"He was chasing me, sir, and I tripped on them old cobblestones under the Buttercross."

"Who was chasing you? Nathaniel Martyn?"

"No, sir. The constable, after Mr Nathaniel told him I was thieving."

"But you weren't."

"No, sir. I was not."

Jacob and the doctor exchanged glances. Jacob felt the next move was his, so he said, "Sarah has not been in my household for long, doctor, but I have found her to be honest. I wouldn't keep her on if she weren't, since as you know, I often have valuable items belonging to my customers in the house while I'm working on them."

He didn't feel it necessary to enlighten Sheridan as to Sarah's semi-criminal past or her talents as a pickpocket. It was possible he was already aware of those.

"I see." Sheridan seemed to be debating with himself whether to believe either of them.

"Thank you for treating her, doctor," Jacob added. "She must have sustained quite a blow when she fell."

"Considerable bruising and the skin was badly grazed," Sheridan said, reverting promptly to his professional manner. "It bled profusely at first. I staunched the bleeding and applied an ointment, then the bandage. She should keep that on until evening, and then change it for a clean one. I'll send one with her."

"Yes, doctor," Sarah murmured.

Sheridan turned to her. "And if you should feel light-headed or faint, sit down until it passes. You don't want to risk injuring yourself further by falling a second time."

"No, sir."

"The wound should heal by itself in a few days, but keep it clean and if there is any sign of infection, come back to see me."

"Yes, sir."

Sarah started to stand up, but wavered and grasped the back of the chair to keep her balance.

"Sit down," Sheridan ordered her. "I am not expecting any more patients for a while, so you will be better off here for the time being."

He went to the door of the examination room and Jacob heard him say, "A cup of strong, sweet tea, please."

Sarah sank back down on the chair. Her face was still pale and Jacob began to wonder how he could get her back safely to his own house. It was only a quarter of a mile or so, but that was a long way to walk for someone in her condition. He could hardly expect Sheridan to offer the horse and trap he used for calling on patients, and Jacob's only method of transport was his own two feet.

He was still pondering this when the housekeeper appeared with a cup of hot tea and handed it to Sarah, who took it and said politely, "Thank you, ma'am."

Sheridan watched her warily, as if expecting her to suddenly throw the cup down and bolt from the room. Jacob felt he should say something, if only to emphasize his gratitude, but to his astonishment he heard himself asking, "Dr Sheridan, as long as we are here, would you be kind enough to answer a question for me?"

Out of the corner of his eye, he saw Sarah shift on the chair and a look of intense interest creep across her bruised face.

"That depends," Sheridan said. "What is it?"

"As you know, I was in Church Green this morning, on an errand, and I saw you conversing with the two police officers from the station. I assumed from your actions you were discussing Thomas Martyn's death. You asked me about my magnifying glass."

"Yes, I remember."

"I have it with me now, in case you still have need of it."

Sheridan suddenly seemed to give Jacob his full attention.

"You do?"

"Yes."

"And your question?"

Jacob took a deep breath. "I heard you say that you felt Mr Martyn's death might not be strictly an accident. Is it possible for you to tell me why you thought that?"

Sheridan's eyes flickered from Jacob to Sarah, who sat as if frozen on the chair, the untouched cup of tea in her hand.

"I'm under no obligation to explain my conclusions to you, Silver, and certainly not to Miss Simm."

"Of course not. I apologize for asking."

"Why do you want to know?"

Jacob had the sensation of aiming a dart at a target, and hoping to hit the correct area.

He said slowly, "Because Mr Martyn visited me the night before he died, Monday night, that is, and made a very odd request of me. I didn't understand it then and I still don't. But he placed me under a certain obligation and I need to know if his death is connected to that."

Before Sheridan could respond, he added, "And if there is any suspicion that his death was not accidental, I would need to know that, and any other details that are available. I don't ask this lightly, but if I'm able to, I feel I should carry out his wishes."

"I see," Sheridan said. He looked at Sarah. "An obligation, eh?"

"Sarah is aware of the situation," Jacob said. "She heard what Mr Martyn told me."

"Very well." Sheridan took up a stance in front of them. "I have asked that a formal investigation be made into Martyn's death, and I understand a police inspector from London will be arriving shortly to direct it. I requested this as a result of my observations when I examined Martyn's body."

Jacob waited patiently while the doctor marshaled his thoughts. He also appeared – understandably – to be debating how much information to share with two people with no civic authority, and who dwelt on the fringes of acceptable society.

"Thomas Martyn died as a result of extensive blood loss," Sheridan said finally. "There was a deep wound in his chest, piercing the heart."

He glanced at Sarah, presumably to see if this information was too graphic for a young woman's delicate constitution. Sarah gazed back at him with wide blue eyes, totally unbothered. Sheridan cleared his throat and continued.

"It was generally assumed he died as a result of being crushed by the falling branch, and there were bloodstains on the branch, corresponding roughly to the same place on his chest where it had landed. Of course, it may have been shifted somewhat when the police were trying to reach the body."

Jacob nodded, to show he was following the doctor's explanation. Sarah sipped her tea and he noticed the color was coming back into her face.

"However," Sheridan said, "there was nothing on the branch at that point – no sharp ends of wood or splintered bark – which could have inflicted such a deep wound. The bloodstains were on a perfectly smooth section of bark, and as far as I could observe, on that section only. So the wound must have been made previously by some other sharper object, such as a knife blade, and then the branch dragged over it in the hope that blood would seep onto it and that would be accepted as the cause of death. Are you a gambling man, Silver?"

"I'm afraid I can't afford to be, sir," Jacob said with a smile.

"No, I suppose not. Even so, I am sure you can appreciate the odds against a sharp bit of wood from a branch landing in precisely the right place to inflict a fatal injury of this type. And that is assuming a severe wind storm would occur at the opportune time to make such a branch fall on a man who just happened to be standing under it and who did not move when he heard a large branch crack overhead.

"Of course, a police surgeon will be sent from London and will no doubt make his own examination of the injuries, but I expect that his findings will confirm my own. Do you now see why I insisted that a full inquiry be made into Thomas Martyn's death?"

NINE

"Absolutely, sir," Jacob said. "You are entirely justified to ask for it."

"You say that, but the Martyn family, of course, are not at all pleased about an investigation being conducted. They would naturally prefer to think his death was a tragic accident."

"Yes, I can see that they would."

"But it is my considered opinion that his death resulted from a stab wound of some sort, not by being crushed."

"Was his ribs broken?" Sarah asked calmly.

Sheridan shot her a glance which was almost appreciative.

"No, they were not. I found no broken bones at all."

"Adding still more weight to your theory," Jacob said. "I saw the branch, as did Sarah, so we know how large and heavy it was."

"Exactly," Sheridan said. "If it had fallen on him from a great height, it certainly would have caused more damage to his chest and perhaps other parts of his body. I believe someone dragged or shifted the fallen branch once Martyn was dead, at least enough to cover the original wound. Unfortunately, death had occurred several hours before I examined the body and I could not give an estimate as to when that might have been, at least not a precise one."

"It was after the wind got up, anyway," Sarah said. "If that happened like you said, sir, then the branch must have been already on the ground, and that gave whoever stabbed him the idea of how to hide the place the knife went in."

"Miss Simm," Sheridan said, "you are altogether too observant for a housemaid. And furthermore, I'm sure you are correct."

Sarah turned pink with either pleasure or embarrassment – Jacob wasn't sure which. He said, "How was Mr Martyn dressed when you first saw him, Doctor? Or perhaps I should ask, was he dressed for an extended outing in foul weather, or in clothes indicating he had just stepped out of his house for a moment, perhaps to speak to someone he didn't intend to admit?"

Sheridan's eyebrows shot up.

"An excellent point. He was wearing a jacket, but not a heavy coat or a hat, so I would say the latter. I am grateful to you for raising the question and I will mention it to the inspector when he arrives."

The three of them sat in silence for a moment and then the doctor said, "I have shared my information with you, Silver, so now it is time for you to pay the piper."

"Sir?"

"What is the obligation Thomas Martyn placed you under?"

Jacob hesitated, remembering Martyn's haunted expression as he gave him the watch.

"You do realize," Sheridan added, "that if Martyn was murdered, as I believe he was, there must have been a compelling reason for someone to do so. At least I find it hard to believe he was stabbed during a raging storm by a casual passer-by, who then went to so much trouble to disguise his crime. If the obligation you speak of has anything to do with the reason he was murdered, the police inspector will need to know about it."

"Yes, of course." Jacob looked at Sarah, who for once seemed unable or unwilling to share her opinion. He sighed.

"Mr Martyn asked me to look after something, as it happened, an item I had recently repaired for him. He

88

specifically told me not to let anyone know I had it and not to give it to anyone else. So I am already breaking my word by telling you of it."

Sheridan nodded, his eyes fixed on Jacob. "I assure you, Silver, your confidence is safe with me. Was this item valuable?"

"Very valuable. And a family heirloom as well."

"How interesting."

"Of course, it may have no connection to his death," Jacob said. "But when he came to see me, he appeared ... agitated. Whatever was worrying him, it obviously was weighing heavily on his mind. He told me he might be wrong about something and if so, he would return and reclaim the item. I agreed to keep it for him, not that he gave me much choice. And then, little more than twenty-four hours later, he was dead."

"So he weren't wrong," Sarah said.

"It would appear not," Sheridan said drily. "But he gave you no clue as to what he was referring to, the subject that was worrying him?"

"None at all."

It was nearly an hour later when Jacob and Sarah returned to the little house in Corn Street. Sarah had recovered somewhat, although she still winced with every step, and Jacob had thrown caution aside and offered her his arm to lean on as they walked. He was far past caring what the townspeople might think as they made their way down the street, drawing curious stares and no doubt speculation as to the nature of their relationship.

By mutual unspoken consent, neither of them had told Sheridan about Nathaniel's visit to the workshop with the constable, but Jacob felt obliged to mention it as they walked along.

"I wonder if we shall have to tell the police about Nathaniel Martyn's accusation when he came to the house, even though your quick thinking kept him from finding the watch."

"Shouldn't think so, sir. He hates me already, that Mr Nathaniel. No point making things worse."

Jacob, acutely aware that he had broken his word to Martyn by telling the doctor about his request, could only agree. His only justification was that if Sheridan would hardly have insisted on an official investigation of Martyn's death if he had been involved in causing it, or in covering it up. Everyone else seemed prepared to believe the falling branch and bad luck theory, which undoubtedly had been what Martyn's killer had been hoping for.

"If Nathaniel says anything about it, we may have to tell them."

"He won't," Sarah said confidently, as they reached the front door. "It'd make him look more of a fool if he did."

Jacob hoped sincerely that she was right. He told Sarah to sit down on a kitchen chair while he looked around to see what he could find for their evening meal. The cupboards were depressingly bare, but he managed to locate cheese and bread, which he placed on the table between them, along with some onion chutney. It was just as well, he reflected, that neither of them had much of an appetite after the events of the day.

He made a pot of tea and poured a cup for each of them. When they had finished the food and drunk the tea, Jacob said, "I suppose I should ask if you really were only talking to the Martyns' kitchen maid. Gracie, is it?"

"Don't you believe me, Mr Silver?"

"I'd like to believe you."

"Not quite the same, is it? But I was, honest."

"Good. I apologize for doubting you. Did you learn anything from her?" He took it as given that Thomas Martyn's death had been the main topic of conversation.

Sarah nodded. "Proper upset, the whole household was. I mean, it's hard for anyone to do their work when the mistress is havin' an attack of the vapors and Mr Nathaniel's stampin' around blamin' everybody for everything and there's lots of talk going around as to what happened and what they're going to do next. Can't even plan the funeral, from what I hear, 'cause the police are callin' in some inspector and a doctor from London, like Dr Sheridan said, and they can't let him be buried until they've had a look at him. Gracie, she said if Mr Thomas had had any consideration for anybody, he'd have died peaceful in his bed like a Christian and not caused all this bother."

She shot Jacob an apologetic look. "Sorry, sir."

"It's all right, Sarah; I'm not offended. So what made Nathaniel think you had stolen anything from the kitchen?"

"Don't rightly know. I was halfway across Church Green and all of a sudden I saw the constable comin' after me with his truncheon out and I ran."

"Possibly not the best course of action."

"I guess not, 'cause I caught my boot heel in those old stones under the Buttercross and fell over."

"No, I meant it wasn't wise because it made you look as if you were guilty of something."

Sarah considered this. "See what you mean, sir. But you can't be guilty of something if they can't get hold of you, either."

Jacob doubted this was true. But he knew from experience that reasoning with Sarah was like trying to catch hold of a slippery eel, so he said, "Who sent for the doctor?"

"The constable did. Or at least he marched me down to the surgery, not that I could walk very easy. Reckon he didn't want me bleedin' all over his nice clean tunic."

Jacob could just picture the constable dragging or propelling his unwilling charge across the High Street and down to the surgery.

"It appears that at some point he dropped the idea of charging you with theft, though."

"Doctor said he'd take responsibility for me. Don't think the constable liked the idea, but he didn't argue. And Mr Nathaniel, he'd already lost interest."

"I wonder why."

"'Cause he found out nothing was missing?"

"But in that case …" Jacob shook his head. "That doesn't make any sense, Sarah."

"Maybe not, but I ain't going to argue about it. Doctor took me in and the constable went off to tell Mr Nathaniel it was all in hand. He came back just afore you got there – the constable, that is – and said there wouldn't be no more said about it."

"It could be," Jacob said, "that by that time, both Nathaniel and the constable realized they had more important things to worry about."

Sheridan had given Sarah the clean bandage to take home with her, and before she went to bed, Jacob helped her remove the soiled one and replace it. He winced at the sight of the caked blood on it, and marveled that she hadn't been knocked unconscious. If she had been running hard, as he assumed she had been, her fall onto the rough medieval cobblestones would have been a forceful one.

He dropped the bloody bandage into the scullery sink, then took a cloth and dampened it with cold water. He carefully cleaned the area around the wound and wrapped the new bandage snugly around her head.

"Ta, Mr Silver. You'd have made a good doctor."

"I doubt that. Is it very painful?"

"Not too bad. Looks worse than it is, I expect." She put an experimental hand to her head, tapping the injured area with her fingertips.

A suspicion came into Jacob's mind. He tried to dismiss it, but without success.

"Sarah, you didn't trip and fall on purpose, did you? So that I'd be summoned to the surgery?"

She looked up at him from under the bandage, which gave her a vaguely piratical appearance.

"Too clever by half, ain't you, Mr Silver?"

Jacob felt like hitting his own head against a wall. So her injury was genuine enough, but it had been self-inflicted. He was glad he'd been unaware of that when they were at the surgery; it would have been impossible for him to ask any questions of Sheridan if he had known.

"Sarah, you shouldn't have done that," he said sternly. "What were you thinking of? You could have been much more badly injured. Broken bones and who knows what else."

"Didn't mean to fall quite so hard, but it worked, didn't it? All I did was kind of creep out of the kitchen like I was tryin' to hide something, and make sure I caught cook's eye. She must have told the butler and he told Mr Nathaniel and since the constable was already there ... well, I started runnin' but I had to slow down so he could catch me up."

Jacob didn't know whether to continue to scold her or burst out laughing. He doubted either action would accomplish anything and he fought to keep his face straight.

"I imagine I could have engineered a meeting with Dr Sheridan without you resorting to such underhanded, not to mention dangerous, methods," he said, with as much dignity as he could manage. "I appreciate your helpfulness, but honestly, Sarah ..."

He gave up, because Sarah was grinning, and reluctantly, he smiled back.

"It's no good, Mr Silver," she said. "Don't get me wrong; you're ever so clever, but you're too honest and you're almost respectable. You talk proper and you're real polite and long as you don't push too hard, people tell you things. That's all very well, but me, I can do and say things and go places you can't. I knew you was wanting to talk to the doctor and I knew he wouldn't tell me nothin', so I had to get you there somehow."

"At the risk of breaking your neck."

"But it worked, Mr Silver, that's the important bit. You came to the surgery, stepped in there right smartish and asked the right questions and now we know that branch didn't just fall off and crush Mr Martyn. Somebody stabbed him first."

Despite himself, Jacob felt a small glow of pride at her praise. Sarah was continuing.

"So I reckon, you and me, together we can work out who killed Mr Martyn and why they done it."

She paused.

"Why they *did* it, I mean."

"I believe the police will be doing that, Sarah. With Dr Sheridan's assistance."

"Oh, arr, but wouldn't it be good if we could work it out first? Then you wouldn't have to tell them about that watch at all."

She looked hopeful and Jacob realized she was envisioning some sort of unholy alliance, two outsiders skirting around the edges of the official inquiry and picking up facts and impressions with which to resolve the mystery of Thomas Martyn's murder before the police eventually arrived at the truth. That was bad enough, but to his consternation, he found the idea appealing.

Before he could let it take hold too deeply, he said, "We'll see what happens tomorrow. Go to bed now, Sarah. I'm sure you need to rest after such an exhausting experience."

"Reckon I do, sir. I've got a bit of a headache."

"You're very fortunate if that's all you've got. Good night, Sarah."

"Good night, Mr Silver. And sir?"

"Yes?"

"Least I made you smile. You don't smile enough."

He could have shot back that there was little to smile about in the current situation, but instead he watched her carefully climb the stairs, holding the rail. It shook him to think she had flung herself onto the cobblestones and risked serious injury simply to learn a little more about Thomas Martyn's death. Thomas Martyn's *murder*, he corrected himself, and whether or not he liked it, he himself was involved, more deeply than she was.

When he was sure Sarah had arrived safely at the top of the stairs, Jacob went into his workshop and unlocked the drawer where he had secreted Martyn's watch. With all that had happened, he wouldn't have been surprised to find it gone, but it was still there, half hidden under a pile of miscellaneous watch parts and a few complete watches that for some reason had been unclaimed by their original owners.

Martyn's gold watch gleamed among them like a polished diamond in a pile of pebbles, and Jacob considered rubbing a little dirt on it by way of disguise. That almost seemed like sacrilege, however, so he compromised by dipping his finger into the coal scuttle and smearing a little dust across the case to dull the luster, taking care not to let it work its way inside and undo his repair work. Then he put it back under the other watches, closed the drawer and locked it.

Jacob was up early the next morning, having decided it would be preferable if Mrs Tucker wasn't faced with a bloody bandage as she entered the scullery. He had also risen once during the night to check on Sarah, opening the box room door a crack and peering through it. She appeared to be sleeping peacefully, the clean bandage still wrapped around her forehead. He had smiled, closed the door and tiptoed back to his own bed.

Down in the scullery, he took the soiled bandage and scrubbed it in a sink of cold water with laundry soap until only a faint pink stain remained. As he wrung it out, he heard Sarah's footsteps on the stairs and then her reproachful voice.

"Oh, Mr Silver, you needn't have done that. I'd have washed it after breakfast."

"I didn't want to frighten Mrs Tucker into fits. How are you feeling this morning?"

She peered at him from under the bandage, which had slipped over one eye. "A bit sore, sir, but not too poorly."

Jacob regarded her critically and said, "Please don't pretend to feel better than you do, Sarah. There's no point in that. On the other hand, I think Dr Sheridan will become suspicious if you appear too often in his surgery. So I'll ask you again, expecting an honest answer; how are you feeling?"

"I'm all right, sir. I'll make the tea now and boil you an egg."

She slipped into the kitchen and Jacob hung the wet bandage on the overhead rack. He was drying his hands when Mrs Tucker hove into sight.

"Mr Silver, whatever are you doing? Where's that girl? Washing's her job, not yours."

"She sustained an injury yesterday, Mrs Tucker. I was merely washing the bandage she used."

"Bandage? Injury? What's she been doing to herself?"

Jacob opened his mouth to answer, but was forestalled by Sarah's appearance in the doorway. She had tightened the bandage so it no longer fell over her eye, but the effect was still startling.

"Mornin', Mrs Tucker," she said. "Your tea's ready, Mr Silver, and when you've had it and a bit of breakfast, I reckon we should get started on our work, don't you?"

TEN

Jacob didn't expect that comment to go unchallenged by Mrs Tucker, and he wasn't disappointed. She drew herself up, hands on ample hips, and addressed Sarah.

"Since when do you give the orders in this house? Beggin' your pardon, Mr Silver, but it ain't her place to tell you what to do, now is it?"

"No, it's not," he said firmly. "Sarah, finish cooking breakfast, and then we will discuss the day's activities. Mrs Tucker, would you like to sit down and have a cup of tea before you start work?"

"Thank you, sir, I would. It's a fair walk here and I'm not as young as I was."

Mollified, Mrs Tucker trundled into the kitchen and sat at the table, waiting for Sarah to pour her tea. Behind her back, Jacob caught Sarah's eye and shook his head slightly. She nodded and turned to the stove, where she was boiling an egg for him.

"There you are, Mrs Tucker, nice and hot," she said, depositing a cup of tea on the table.

"Ta."

Jacob waited patiently while she drank it before sitting down with his own breakfast. Unlike Sarah, Mrs Tucker had a strong sense of the fitness of things, and wouldn't have dreamed of sharing the table with him, even for a cup of tea. Eventually she stood up and went off to the scullery with a last disapproving look at Sarah.

Jacob sliced the top off his egg and dug into the yolk. Sarah hovered nearby.

"Don't reckon I can go into town, not 'til I get this bandage off," she said. "Looks like I've been fightin' and someone gave me a good thump."

Jacob felt that engaging in a street brawl probably would be well within her capabilities, given her personality, but he had to agree.

"No, let Mrs Tucker do the marketing today," he said. "There's work to be done here, I'm sure."

"Rugs need beating," Sarah said. "I can do that while she's out."

"That's a good idea. I'll leave you two to divide up your duties."

He made a hasty escape to his workshop, trying to ignore the fragments of conversation that drifted back to him. The general theme seemed to be that Sarah had been very clumsy and was fortunate not to have been either killed or dismissed from her post. From Mrs Tucker's tones, she regarded the two alternatives in much the same light.

Eventually he heard the scullery door close and a moment later Mrs Tucker's solid figure passed by Jacob's window, the marketing basket swinging from her arm. A series of rhythmic thuds from the back of the house told him Sarah was carrying out her plan to beat the rugs.

By the time Mrs Tucker returned, Sarah had replaced the rugs and Jacob had recalibrated another watch. He rubbed his eyes tiredly, since the close work inevitably strained them and sometimes gave him a headache as well. There were times he wondered how long he could keep doing this work, and what would happen when he couldn't. That in turn made him think of Thomas and Nathaniel Martyn and the Martyns' factory, and what its future prospects were if Nathaniel were to be placed in charge. He got down from his stool and went to the kitchen to see if Mrs Tucker had picked up any gossip along with the fish and vegetables.

He opened the door just in time to hear her say, "… shouldn't be surprised if he did."

"Shouldn't be surprised if who did what?" he asked.

"Don't want you thinking I've been gossiping, Mr Silver," Mrs Tucker said defensively, "but there's a police inspector and some special doctor coming all the way from London on account of Mr Martyn's death, 'cause them constables here think there's something a bit odd about it, and people are saying Jerome Mead might have done something to him."

Jacob thought it over. Her report of the main fact was correct, but it had been Dr Sheridan rather than the constable and sergeant who had instigated the London inspector and police surgeon's visit, and apparently no one but those three knew about the knife wound in Martyn's chest. No one but those three, himself and Sarah, that is.

"I thought he was hit and killed by a falling tree branch," he said, trying to sound both innocent and unconcerned.

"He was, sir, but for some reason them constables ain't happy with that. It's said Mead was threatening to kill Mr Martyn and then he turned up dead, so what were they to think?"

What, indeed, Jacob thought. As far as he knew, there was no solid evidence tying Jerome Mead to Martyn's death, but the future didn't look bright for Mead, regardless of whether he was actually guilty.

Sarah stirred in the doorway and said, "So when's this high and mighty London police inspector coming here?"

"Him and the doctor's expected on the midday train," Mrs Tucker said, obviously proud of having this news to relay.

Jacob thought he could see Sarah thinking of an excuse to be in the vicinity of the railway station at midday. To dampen her enthusiasm, he said, "I imagine Sergeant Bell will meet them and give them all the information he has."

"Oh, arr. Just that I ain't never seen a real police inspector or a special police doctor, only them two in Church Green."

"They will probably look much like anyone else," Jacob said, deciding not to comment that Sarah had seen far too much of the local constabulary lately. "And if they're in town long, I expect you'll get a glimpse of them."

Disappointment showed plainly on her face, but he knew she wouldn't argue with him in front of Mrs Tucker.

"So I'll be on my way," Mrs Tucker said. "There's potatoes, carrots and a nice bit of mutton for your supper, Mr Silver, if she'll be up to cookin' it, what with that knock on the head she got."

"Course I will," Sarah said. She turned on her heel and went back through the doorway, while Mrs Tucker settled her shawl around her shoulders and followed her into the scullery.

Once he was certain she'd gone, Jacob put his head through the scullery door.

"Sarah?"

"Sir?"

"I hope I made myself clear. I don't want to see you at the railway station when the inspector and surgeon arrive."

"No, sir. Does that mean you'll be there, Mr Silver, when you won't be seeing me?"

"I may be," Jacob said. "I have to take a necklace and a bill to a customer in Cogges."

"So if you go now, you should be passing by the station just about midday, maybe?"

"Quite possibly."

"D'ye think you'll get a chance to talk to them?"

Jacob lifted his eyebrows. "What would I talk to them about? I'm not a constable, only a simple craftsman, repairing clocks and jewelry."

"And watches," Sarah said. "Nice gentlemen's watches. Don't forget about those."

It was a calm, sunny day, the wind storm of two days earlier only a memory. Even if he hadn't had an ulterior motive, Jacob would have enjoyed his walk through the town and across the river to Cogges, a hamlet nestled on the far side of the Windrush. The customer's bill was neatly folded in his pocket along with the repaired necklace, providing his excuse, and he walked purposefully, keeping his eyes on the road in front of him so as not to attract unwanted attention.

At two minutes to twelve, he was approaching the new railway station, where of course he would have to stop for a few minutes to allow the scheduled train to pass. He slowed his pace just enough to reach the station as the blast of the whistle and the vibration of wheels on the rails announced its arrival.

The train thundered into the station, belching a cloud of steam and coming to a noisy halt beside the platform. Jacob, waiting patiently for the passengers to disembark and the train to leave so he could cross the rails safely, saw Sergeant Bell striding forward to greet someone.

Despite his words to Sarah, Jacob had somehow expected the inspector to be instantly recognizable, perhaps having an inborn air of command like a general or admiral. The man who alighted from the train was not like that, however, and in fact was closer to Jacob's original prediction of looking much like anyone else.

He was of average height and build, wearing a long-tailed coat and trousers with highly polished boots visible under them. His hat partially covered very ordinary brown hair, and as Jacob's curious gaze rested on his face for a moment, he saw a pair of penetrating blue eyes looking back at him. A man to be reckoned with, Jacob thought, which gave him hope that the inspector would quickly get to the truth of Martyn's murder without involving him.

Another well-dressed man accompanied him, carrying a black leather bag. He was taller, thinner and more self-absorbed, only greeting the local sergeant briefly with a nod and a handshake, and then standing back to let the inspector speak.

Jacob quickly moved on, before Bell could notice him and question why he was there, although a swift backward glance showed him the two police officers were deep in conversation and not watching him. The train pulled out of the station again, and Jacob continued on toward his customer's house.

By the time he had made his delivery and retraced his steps, the train, the sergeant, the inspector and the police surgeon were all long gone. He walked back into the town, crossing the end of Church Green, and saw the two police officers, now joined by the constable and Dr Sheridan, gathered around the spot where Thomas Martyn had died. The surgeon was again standing a pace or two back from the others, silently observing the scene, as was a small knot of curious onlookers.

The branches now had been completely removed, but Sheridan was gesturing, obviously explaining to the inspector where they had been and what he had observed. Jacob's eyes moved to the windows of the Martyn house, where he saw the curtains twitch behind their black veils. No doubt the family members, the servants, or both, were keeping a close eye on proceedings while pretending to be too consumed by grief to notice.

Jacob kept walking, although an observer would have noticed his pace slowing considerably. That meant he was still within sight when Dr Sheridan left the group to head back toward his surgery, accompanied by the police surgeon. The constable crossed the green to the police station and the onlookers dispersed. Sergeant Bell, his look of unease clearly visible even from a distance, walked beside the inspector as he went to the front door of the Martyn house and rang the bell.

Jacob smiled to himself. Nathaniel wouldn't like that, a police inspector from London not only questioning the circumstances of his father's death but worse, calling at the front door as if he were a socially acceptable visitor. He didn't wait to see any more, but increased his pace, walking briskly down Corn Street.

He expected Sarah to be waiting anxiously and smiled to see her ostensibly dusting the small parlor but using it as an excuse to look out the window. She shot into the hallway as he opened the door, her face alight with curiosity.

"Did you see the inspector, sir? What's he like?"

"Yes, I saw him and I have no idea of his character, but I did get an impression of intelligence."

Jacob removed his hat and coat and hung them up, since Sarah was too preoccupied to take them.

"What's he look like?"

"Very ordinary, I'm afraid. He's probably about forty years old, so undoubtedly experienced at his job."

"Oh, arr, and they have all kinds of wicked murders in London, don't they? So he'd know how to go about it."

"No doubt."

"Did he talk to you?"

"No, why would he? But he's spoken to Dr Sheridan already, and the local police. When I last saw him, he was about to speak to the Martyn family, and the police surgeon went off with Dr Sheridan, probably to examine Mr Martyn's body."

"I'll have to see Gracie, then." Sarah put the duster down and wiped her hands on her apron with an air of finality.

Jacob started to object, and then realized there was no good reason to. He also noticed Sarah had removed the bandage and combed her short hair down to cover her injury as much as possible. It still looked as though she had been brawling, but now more as though she'd been the victor, not the vanquished.

"Don't be too long," he said. "And this time, do not aggravate Nathaniel Martyn or anyone else. That trick will only work once."

She gazed at him with innocent blue eyes. "I'm only goin' to buy a bit of ribbon at the haberdasher's. Can't help it if I happen to see Gracie on my way."

Jacob knew the haberdashery was only a few doors away from the Martyns' home and silently applauded her ability to come up with a good excuse to be in the neighborhood.

"But housemaids don't wear frivolous things like ribbons and I certainly don't," he said, handing her a few pennies. "You'd be better off buying some buttons to sew on my shirts. And buy them before you see Gracie. It will be more believable that way."

"That's very good thinking, Mr Silver," she said approvingly. "Make a proper villain of you yet."

"Sarah," Jacob protested, then realized she was teasing him. Again. He spared a thought for what his stern, hard-working father would think of his son sharing a joke with a young housemaid and decided it was a good thing he would never know.

"All right, off you go," he said.

Sarah returned an hour later, bubbling with news. Jacob was pleased to see she had found time to purchase half a dozen shirt buttons, since as she had noted, a good cover story was far more believable when backed up with proof.

"The butler heard a lot of what was said and he told the housekeeper and Gracie just happened to be doin' some ironing where she could listen to them talkin' about it. The inspector, his name's Carey, Inspector Carey, that is, and he told Mr Nathaniel that it don't look like an accident. And of course Mr Nathaniel wasn't havin' that and started shouting that he wouldn't stand for the family name bein' dragged through the mud but Inspector Carey told him to calm down, they was only after the truth."

"And how did he react to that?"

"Gracie reckons he don't want the truth. He only wants everyone to go away."

"The London visitors, you mean?"

"Oh, arr. But the inspector said they could probably have the funeral before long, as soon as that police doctor's had a look at Mr Martyn at the undertaker's."

Jacob was glad to hear that. He was used to funerals being held as soon as possible after a death, and delay, even when due to suspected murder, seemed disrespectful and made him uneasy. However, he knew Church of England practices were different, and no doubt relatives and friends had to be given time to be notified and to arrive.

"I expect the funeral will be at St Mary's Church," he said.

"Yes, and a very grand one, too, Gracie said. Mr Nathaniel's arranging it. He said he'd be speaking to the vicar as soon as the inspector left. Course the vicar had already been round soon as he knew Mr Martyn was dead to offer his … what's the word, Mr Silver?"

"Condolences, perhaps? Spiritual comfort or support?" Jacob was a little uncertain what Christians did following a death, but some things were universal. He remembered Mrs Rexford saying she would be calling on poor Evangeline Martyn to express her sympathy, and no doubt there had been a steady stream of callers.

"Something like that. Nobody gave me none of those things when Ma died."

Jacob felt a pang of sympathy. He remembered his own desolation, the difficulty of trying to deal with practicalities of death with only minimal help from the small Jewish community in Oxford, at a time when he had barely recovered from his own illness and felt his heart was breaking in half.

"I know how you feel, Sarah."

She looked at him in surprise. "S'pose you do, sir. And the vicar wouldn't have been much good to you, would he?"

Jacob smiled ruefully. "No, he wouldn't have been, although I'm sure he would have meant well. Anyway, I gather we can expect a funeral with pomp and ceremony in a day or two. Anything else?"

"Well, sir, once Mr Nathaniel kind of came round to the idea someone might have killed his pa, he decided it must be Jerome Mead who done it. So he told Inspector Carey to go arrest him, but the inspector says it don't work that way. He's got to have some, what they call evidence first."

"That's right. The inspector can't arrest Mead just because Nathaniel doesn't like him, although it seems several people, including myself, heard him threaten Mr Martyn."

"So that's where they left it, the inspector goin' to call on Jerome Mead and Mr Nathaniel sayin' it was him. There's a funny thing, though."

"What?"

"Could be Gracie didn't hear everything that was said, 'cause she got it kind of third or fourth hand, you might say, but it didn't sound like Mr Nathaniel ever asked the inspector what made him think his pa's death wasn't an accident. And you'd think that's the one thing he'd really want to know."

ELEVEN

"Yes, you would think so," Jacob agreed, "but as you say, Gracie may not have had the whole story. Or perhaps Nathaniel did ask and the inspector wouldn't give him any details."

Sarah nodded. "Could be. Y'know, it's too bad I couldn't get a post with Mrs Martyn. Then I'd be able to find out a lot more." Jacob frowned and she added hastily, "I don't mean I'm going to do that, Mr Silver. I'm happy enough here. Just that it would be kind of helpful."

"I'm glad to hear you don't mean it. Aside from anything else, I don't think you'd fit into a household like that very well, with a housekeeper and cook telling you what to do, not to mention the family members."

"Probably not. Don't know how my ma put up with it, either. She wouldn't never talk about it much, just said she was glad to leave and marry my pa."

Jacob could well imagine that was true. If Sarah's mother had been anything like her daughter, she would have leaped at the chance of having her own home, however humble, rather than dancing attendance on a demanding employer for twelve or more hours a day.

"What was your mother's name?" he asked.

"Anne, but they called her Annie. Annie Porter. Housemaid, she was."

Sarah gazed off into the distance, obviously recalling memories. Jacob, who barely remembered his own mother, didn't disturb her reverie. Finally she shook her head briskly and said, "So if I can't get inside the house by workin' there, we'll have to find things out some other way. Good thing about a big house like that, with someone always comin' and goin', there's plenty of chances."

Jacob started to object, but she overrode him, saying, "And you probably know people living around Church Green or somewhere there who need their clocks fixing. Or you could find some."

"I don't go door to door soliciting trade, Sarah. Usually people come to me, not the other way around. Most people in Witney know about me."

He nearly added, "For better or worse," but stopped himself in time.

"Too true," Sarah said. "I heard about you at the workhouse, before I came here."

"Is that why you picked my house to steal from?"

"No, course not. I didn't know you had anything worth stealin'. It was just 'cause I saw that lovely gold watch sitting there and no one about."

"Opportunistic, then, rather than deliberate."

She made a face, wrinkling her nose. "You're using them big words again, Mr Silver, tryin' to trip me up. But what I meant was, if you was to go up around Church Green, just for a walk, like, or goin' to a shop, somebody might see you and remember they had something needing to be fixed. A clock or some jewelry or something. Like you say, everybody knows you and how good you are at that sort of thing."

"Perhaps the police station clock could conveniently develop a fault as I walked past, and they would call me in to repair it," Jacob said, ignoring the flattery. He meant it as a sarcastic comment, but Sarah took it seriously.

"D'ye think that could happen, sir?"

"No."

"Oh."

"Nor will I be inquiring about emigration to Australia."

A thoughtful look stole over Sarah's face and Jacob said, "No, don't do that. It wouldn't help the situation and may possibly hinder it. However, I have a suggestion."

"Yes?"

He fixed her with a stern glare.

"You defied my orders and went into town this afternoon, despite being advised to stop in the house until your head had healed. I am concerned that you may have developed a fever as a result and I shall consult Dr Sheridan as to the best treatment."

Even as he said it, Jacob wondered how this inquisitive, exasperating girl had led him into a situation where he was contemplating telling a doctor an outright lie, just on the chance that he might learn something about a matter which was probably none of his business. *But it* is *my business*, he protested inwardly, *at least until I discover why Thomas Martyn left that watch with me.*

Sarah, unaware of his internal debate, was pressing her hand to her forehead, a worried expression on her face.

"It does feel a bit hot, sir. You may be right."

"At least that will give me a reason to be in town. If the doctor isn't there, or I come to my senses before I speak to him, then I shall return. It will be time for supper before long, anyway."

Sarah suddenly froze, her hand still pressed to her head.

"Are you all right, Sarah?" Jacob asked, wondering if the fabricated fever could possibly be a reality.

"Oh, arr." She lowered her hand. "Looks like you may not have to think of a reason to go into town after all."

She had been looking past him to the front window and Jacob whirled around. Through the glass he could see two figures standing at his gate. One was the local sergeant, and the other was Inspector Carey.

Jacob fought down a feeling of panic. It was one thing to be unjustly suspected of theft by a local constable, but quite another to have a London police inspector on the doorstep. He told himself to calm down because he'd done nothing wrong, and shot a quick glance at Sarah.

"Tell the truth if he asks you any questions," he said quietly. "If you lie, it will catch up with you later."

"Even about me falling down, sir?"

"Within reason."

The constable rapped on the door and Jacob went to answer it, Sarah a pace or two behind him.

"Jacob Silver?" the inspector inquired.

"Yes, sir."

"I'm Police Inspector Owen Carey. I believe you know Sergeant Bell."

"Yes, I do, by reputation, anyway. Will you both come in?"

"Thank you."

The two police officers came into the hallway and Jacob, after a moment's hesitation – and remembering that Sarah had dusted it earlier – opened the door to the little-used parlor and invited them to sit down. Sarah hovered in the hallway behind them, obviously torn between wanting to eavesdrop and a desire to avoid the sergeant's attention.

"May I offer you a cup of tea?" Jacob asked.

"No, thank you," Carey said, although Bell looked as though he would have happily accepted.

With some reluctance, Jacob closed the door, knowing Sarah would have been delighted to serve them tea, and even now, probably had her ear pressed to the keyhole.

Carey cleared his throat and Bell took out a notebook and pen. Jacob sat to attention and waited.

"As you may be aware, Mr Silver," the inspector began, "a prominent Witney citizen, Mr Thomas Martyn, died on Tuesday evening. I have been called in from London by the local constabulary to investigate the circumstances of his death."

Jacob nodded politely. "Yes, I understand."

"Part of my investigation includes speaking to anyone who had contact with Mr Martyn on the day of his death. I am told you spoke to him at his factory on Tuesday afternoon. Is that correct?"

Jacob breathed a little easier. If the inspector only wanted to know what had passed between them at that encounter he could tell the truth and not worry about being tripped up or accused of anything. He was curious as to who had reported his presence there, but that could wait. Probably it had been Collins, the large guard at the door.

"Yes, sir," he said.

"Why did you go there?"

"Because I called at his house first and was told he was at the factory."

He hadn't meant his reply to be facetious, but the inspector frowned at him.

"I meant: Why did you want to speak to him?"

"It was concerning a repair I had done for him recently." Jacob felt that was truthful enough.

"It had nothing to do with the factory itself, then?"

"No, sir, not at all. I have no knowledge of factory workings."

"Was anyone else present when you spoke to Mr Martyn?"

"Yes. A man called Collins, whom I believe is an employee of the factory, and another man whose role was unclear."

"Do you know his name?"

"I didn't at the time, but Mr Martyn referred to him later as Mr Mead."

Carey looked satisfied at this response and Bell wrote feverishly in his notebook. Jacob wondered how much of the interrogation Sarah could catch. Quite a bit, he supposed.

"Please recount for me, Mr Silver, as accurately as you can, what words passed between Mr Martyn and Mr Mead."

Jacob closed his eyes for a moment, trying to recall the exact words, but it was no good. He could only remember his own attempts to tell Martyn about Nathaniel's actions without stating them outright.

"I don't remember the precise words, I'm afraid, but the general idea was that Mr Mead was trying to persuade Mr Martyn to change his mind about something and Mr Martyn was insisting that he had taken his decision and would not budge. And before you ask, I have no idea at all what they were referring to. Given the location, I assumed it had something to do with the factory, but I could be wrong."

"How would you describe Mr Mead's tone of voice?"

"I would say irritable, verging on angry."

"And Mr Martyn's?"

Jacob smiled slightly. "Stubborn. It was clear, to me at least, he would not be moved."

"Did Mr Mead make any threats?"

"I suppose it could be taken that way. As I recall, he stated that if Mr Martyn did not change his mind on whatever matter they were discussing, that he would regret it."

Bell wrote this down without comment, leading Jacob to think they had already spoken to the servants and received a similar account of the meeting between the two men at the house. The animosity between them was not exactly a secret.

"How did their conversation end?" Carey asked.

A few words flashed back into Jacob's memory. "I believe Mr Martyn said that 'violence would be met with violence'. And then Mr Mead turned and left the factory."

"And that was all?"

"Yes, sir."

"Were you able to consult Mr Martyn on the matter which had taken you there?"

"Yes, I was."

"Satisfactorily?"

An honest answer would have been negative, but Jacob decided that wouldn't be prudent.

"Yes, sir."

"Did you see Mr Mead on any other occasion?"

"No, sir."

Bell made some more notes and Jacob allowed himself to relax slightly.

"Mr Silver, are you acquainted with Thomas Martyn's son, Nathaniel?"

The sense of safety Jacob felt was immediately washed away by apprehension.

"Not to say acquainted, sir. We have never actually been introduced, but I have seen him briefly."

"Where?"

Jacob's mind raced. Did the inspector know that Nathaniel had accused him of stealing the watch and brought the constable to search for it? Since the accusation had failed for lack of evidence, an honest answer might be advisable.

"Once at his father's house, and once here at my workshop."

"Did he accuse you of theft on either occasion?"

So the inspector had been told by the constable about the abortive visit.

"Yes, sir, he did. Unjustly, I may say."

To Jacob's amazement, the inspector smiled, his expression indicating that Nathaniel had made much the same first impression on Carey as he had on Jacob.

"So I've been told. And you have had no other communication with Nathaniel Martyn?"

"None at all."

"When you spoke to Mr Martyn at the factory on Tuesday, did he give any indication of his plans for the remainder of the day, or the evening?"

"No, sir." Jacob was silently amused that the inspector would think Martyn would confide in him. Surely he had questioned the man's wife and servants, who would have a far better chance of knowing why Martyn had left the house that night in a raging windstorm. Perhaps he had, and was now clutching at straws.

"And yourself, Mr Silver, where were you on Tuesday evening?"

"Here, at my house."

"Can anyone confirm that?"

"Yes, up until about nine o'clock. Not after that, but I didn't leave the house."

Carey looked at some notes. "Do you employ a housemaid called Sarah Simm?"

Jacob gulped, wondering in what context the inspector had learned Sarah's name. "Yes, sir, I do."

"May I speak with her, please? If you wish your wife or another woman to be present, that is quite in order."

"I am a widower, Inspector, and my housekeeper is only here for a few hours a day. I think Sarah will be quite capable of speaking to you on her own. Shall I fetch her?"

He hoped Sarah had taken the opportunity during his response to retreat from her listening post. It would be embarrassing, to say the least, to open the parlor door and have her tumble inside.

"Please."

Jacob stood up and went to the door, relieved not to find Sarah crouching outside it. She was in the kitchen doorway, her face displaying a neat combination of excitement and concern.

"Inspector Carey wishes to speak to you, Sarah," he said, a little louder than necessary. "I'm sure it is merely a few questions, nothing to worry about."

"No, sir."

Their eyes met and Sarah nodded to show she had heard everything he had said to Carey and Bell. She followed him back to the parlor and sat demurely on a chair, hands folded in her lap, turning innocent blue eyes on the inspector. Since no one had asked Jacob to leave, he stationed himself discreetly in the corner behind her chair.

"Miss Simm, I have just a few questions for you," Carey said. "All you need to do is answer them honestly. Do you understand?"

"Yes, sir."

"How long have you been employed by Mr Silver?"

"About a month, sir, perhaps a little longer."

"And before that?"

"I was in the workhouse, sir, after my ma died."

"So this is your first post."

"Yes, sir."

"You have never had a position, for example, at the home of Thomas Martyn?"

"No, sir."

"I expect you have heard of his death. Were you acquainted with Mr Martyn?"

"No, sir." Sarah twitched slightly in her chair.

"What is it?"

"If you go asking people, sir, you'll find out, so I'll save you the trouble. My ma worked in his house, 'fore she got married. About fifteen years ago, I guess that'd be. So I sort of knew *about* him, even though I didn't know him, if you see what I mean."

"I see," Carey said. "Do you know his son, Nathaniel, or his daughter, Charlotte?"

"No, sir. I mean, again, I know who they are, but I can't say as I know them as people."

She gave Carey a shy, tentative smile, indicating he should understand without being told that a lowly housemaid wouldn't be socially acquainted with the son and daughter of one of the town's most prominent citizens.

"And that has been your only contact with the Martyn household, the fact that your mother was once employed there?"

"Yes, sir."

"Are you certain?"

Sarah's eyebrows went up slightly. "Yes, sir."

"But you have been seen recently outside the tradesmen's door of the house, and even in the kitchen. Or are my witnesses mistaken?"

"Oh, that." Sarah gave a girlish giggle, one which Jacob felt was manufactured for the occasion. "I was just passin' the time of day with one of the housemaids I know. Nothin' to do with the family at all. She won't get into trouble for talking to me, will she?"

Carey gave her a long, stern look, as if to convey that housemaids should tend to their work and not gossip with passers-by. But to Jacob's ears, her explanation sounded reasonable, and apparently the inspector felt the same.

"Any disciplinary measures will be down to Mrs Martyn, and I imagine she is too occupied at the moment to worry about a bit of gossip," Carey said. "But I would advise you, Miss Simm, to stay away from the house in future."

"Yes, sir," Sarah said, and Jacob was sure he saw the possibility of the errand boy Fred calling on Gracie before long. He wondered if she was aware of Sarah's alter ego and whether, like Sarah, she thought it a good joke.

Carey looked over his notes and then back up at Jacob and Sarah.

"How did you learn of Mr Martyn's death?"

Sarah answered quickly, before Jacob could formulate a reply.

"Mr Silver sent me to do the marketing that morning, sir, and I saw a crowd of people standin' about on Church Green, so I went over to see what they was all lookin' at. Everybody was saying as how Mr Martyn had been killed by a falling branch during that dreadful windstorm the night before, so I came right back to the house and told Mr Silver."

"Why?"

Sarah's face registered puzzlement. "I'm sorry, sir?"

"Why did you rush back to tell Mr Silver the news?"

"'Cause it *was* news, sir," she said, looking at Carey as if he were lacking in intelligence. "Exciting, like, in a sad sort of way. I expect you have things like that happening all the time in London, but we don't, not out here. I thought Mr Silver'd be interested, so I came back to tell him."

"And were you interested?" Carey asked Jacob.

"Only as much as any other citizen would be," Jacob said, "Mr Martyn was a customer of mine, and of course, as Sarah says, his death seems to have been rather dramatic."

He waited, thinking Carey might use the opportunity to announce that Martyn's death was not only dramatic but far from accidental. Just when he had given up hope, Carey put his notes away and Bell closed his book with a decisive snap.

"Yes, it was dramatic," Carey said, meeting Jacob's eyes. "And I'm sure you are wondering why it is being investigated by a London police inspector. Unless, of course, you are already aware that it appears to be murder."

TWELVE

Jacob wasn't sure if that statement was meant as an accusation, but it sounded uncomfortably like one. Had Dr Sheridan told the inspector about their visit to the surgery? Or did Carey think Jacob and Sarah had some other source of confidential information? Surely he didn't think either of them could be considered suspects, although Jacob was aware there were quite a few people in the town who would not be either surprised or concerned if they were. He waited to see if more was forthcoming.

"I have been speaking to Dr Sheridan," Carey said, allowing Jacob to breathe again. "He mentioned he had spoken to you and that you and Miss Simm were aware Mr Martyn's death was likely not an accident."

"Yes, sir," Jacob said.

"He also, undoubtedly, told you not to share that information with anyone."

"Not in so many words, but of course we understand we mustn't say anything about it whilst your investigation is taking place."

"Good. And Miss Simm, do you understand this, too?"

"Yes, sir."

"He seems to think the two of you possess not only intelligence but also curiosity and an ability to process information and draw conclusions. Those are admirable traits, but I trust you will keep them under control and leave the investigation to the police, namely, myself."

Jacob swallowed and said, "Yes, sir, we will."

"I think that will be all, then. Thank you both for your assistance."

"I hope it has been helpful."

"It has basically confirmed what I had already been told, but that in itself can be valuable. Obviously, if you should remember anything else of interest, you can reach me through the police station."

"Yes, sir."

Carey stood up and shook hands with Jacob, gave Sarah a brief smile and went out. Bell followed, allowing himself a quick peek into the workshop as he passed the open door. Jacob wondered what he expected to see there – gold ducats stacked in a corner, perhaps. He was glad he had put Martyn's watch into a locked drawer.

He closed the front door behind the two policemen and turned to Sarah.

"That went all right, sir, didn't it?" she said brightly.

"As well as could be expected, I think. At least it appears the inspector doesn't think either of us could be responsible for Martyn's death."

"And didn't the doctor say some nice things about us?"

"I would consider that a mixed blessing, I think."

"So what we need to find out," she went on, "is why Mr Martyn went out that night. Seems he didn't tell anybody, 'cause they would have asked his wife and the butler and if they don't know, then nobody does."

"And how, exactly, do you intend that we should find out information a London police inspector hasn't been able to discern, especially when we have been specifically advised not to meddle?"

"Not you, Mr Silver. I'll do it. I'll think about it tonight, and maybe tomorrow I'll have an idea."

"As long as it doesn't involve hurling yourself onto cobblestones."

"It won't. Now, there's cold mutton and applesauce in the kitchen, and I can do some vegetables – would you like that for your supper?"

"Yes, that sounds fine. And Sarah?"

"Yes, sir?"

"I hope you noted one thing that Inspector Carey failed to mention."

Sarah smiled at him. "Course I did. He never said nothing about Mr Martyn leaving anything with you, so I guess Dr Sheridan didn't tell him that part. I'll get the supper now."

Jacob wasn't entirely certain he wanted to know what Sarah's plan was, but he woke in the morning to the scent of tea and freshly baked bread, which meant that she must have been up for two or three hours and probably had used the time to work out the details. He stopped himself from groaning as he remembered the session with Carey, the double-sided compliment from Sheridan and the way Sarah had taken it for granted that they could find information the inspector couldn't.

Other housemaids busied themselves with cooking, cleaning and washing; he had the bad luck to have acquired one who fancied herself a detective. On that worrying note, he made his way downstairs to see what disasters awaited him.

He found no disaster, but no Sarah, either. Two golden-brown loaves of bread were waiting under their cloths, still warm to the touch, and a pot of tea was keeping hot on the stove. Jacob looked in the parlor, the scullery and even the garden, thick with the acrid smell of early morning coal fires, but he appeared to be the only occupant of the house. He returned to the kitchen to cut himself some bread, butter it and pour a cup of tea, hoping not to be summoned to either the surgery or the police station to retrieve his employee.

He had finished his breakfast and gone into the workshop when Sarah came in. He heard her light footsteps in the kitchen – so different from Mrs Tucker's heavy tread – and then she put her head through the workshop door.

"Morning, Mr Silver. Did you find the bread and tea all right?"

"Yes, I did. Thank you. Where have you been?"

"Talkin' to some people. Had to get up real early to catch them 'fore they went to sleep."

Jacob couldn't make immediate sense of that explanation, and the more he considered it, the less sure he was that he wanted to.

"They're no one you'd know," Sarah said quickly. "At least, I hope you don't know them, not personal like."

Jacob laid down his calipers. "I take it these people are engaged in … questionable … activities."

"S'pose you'd say so. But people got to eat, don't they?"

"Yes. Who are they?"

"Some girls who were out working the street the night of the storm. Easy to remember, 'cause the weather was so bad, so there weren't many punters about." Before Jacob could comment, she continued, "I ain't never done anything like that, Mr Silver, in case you was thinking I had."

"I'm very glad to hear that. I assume you were asking them about Thomas Martyn, whether they'd seen him that night."

"Oh, arr. And it would've been real useful if he'd been one of their regulars, but he weren't. Wasn't, I mean. They know who he is, but he don't use them."

Jacob didn't know whether or not to be relieved at this statement.

"So if he met with someone that night, it wasn't an encounter with a prostitute."

"Seems not, sir, unless he was a long way from his house, and he weren't dressed for that."

"Did you ask them if they saw him at all – going somewhere else, perhaps?"

"I did, and no one saw him. Least not on Church Green, down Corn Street or round Market Square."

"But we do know he was out that night, and probably on foot, even if he only went a short distance from his front door, which seems likely judging from the way he was dressed. However, I wonder if he was attacked as he started out to some other nearby place, or on his return from it. The Buttercross, for example, is no more than a hundred yards or so from his house, and he could have arranged to meet someone there."

"You mean, did someone know he'd be going out and was waitin' for him, or did they follow him back after they'd had their meeting or whatever and stab him outside the door?"

"Exactly. There may have even been two people involved, one to lure him outside on some pretext and another waiting to ambush him."

Sarah tipped her head to one side, a sure sign she was thinking furiously.

"The way he was lying on the ground, he was on his back, with his head toward the door. So maybe he was just leavin'."

"I don't think we can assume that. He could have turned around to face his attacker."

Sarah nodded in agreement and was about to add a comment when they both heard Mrs Tucker opening the scullery door.

"We'll discuss this later," Jacob said, and Sarah hurried into the kitchen. A moment later, he heard them discussing the housework to be done that day, and Mrs Tucker inspecting the bread and grudgingly admitting that Sarah's baking skills were acceptable.

He left them to their tasks and went into his workshop, but he found he couldn't keep his mind on his work. The vision of Thomas Martyn pinned under the fallen branch kept reappearing, even though he hadn't seen it himself. He wondered how Nathaniel was coping with his father's sudden death – would it prompt a new, belated maturity in the young man? And he wondered what was happening at the family's factory, whether the workers would be given time off and expected to attend their employer's funeral, or if it would be business as usual. Since the factory normally operated seven days a week, he imagined it would be the latter.

Jacob finally decided that since he couldn't concentrate on the clock he was attempting to repair, he might as well take Sarah's earlier suggestion and walk into town, hoping to either pick up some information or generate some business. He might even see Inspector Carey again and get some idea of how the investigation was progressing.

He put on his coat and hat, and looked into the scullery, where Mrs Tucker was ironing and Sarah was polishing Jacob's second-best pair of boots.

"I'm going into town for a short while," he told them. "I should be back before midday."

"Yes, sir," Mrs Tucker said.

"Good luck, sir," Sarah said, smothering a yawn.

Jacob walked briskly up Corn Street and paused at the crossroads. He looked across Church Green, mentally estimating the time it would take a man to walk from the Martyn residence to the Buttercross. No more than two or three minutes, he judged, even at night in a storm. There was a flutter of activity at the house in question, with two carriages outside, probably callers expressing their sympathy or relatives arriving.

As Jacob watched, a short, sturdy man dressed in somber black with a clerical collar made his way down the footpath from the direction of St Mary's. So preparations for the grand funeral were also under way. The vicar pulled the bell cord at the front door and was admitted. Jacob moved on.

He had no definite destination in mind, so let his feet dictate his path as he turned left and started toward Market Square. The High Street ran down a slight slope from the square, ultimately leading toward Martyn's factory, and Jacob hoped something would reveal itself before he walked that far. At the least, he could gauge the reaction of the townspeople to Martyn's dramatic death, since reading the mood of the public was a survival lesson he had learned early in life.

As he expected, Martyn's death, Mead's probable guilt and the upcoming funeral were the main topics of conversation. Jacob went briefly into the haberdashery and then the greengrocery, emerging with a handkerchief he didn't need, half a dozen carrots and a rumor that Inspector Carey had been seen at the surgery and was now heading in the direction of the blanket factory. The funeral, he heard, was scheduled for the following afternoon, which must mean that the police surgeon had completed his examination.

He stood on the pavement outside the door of the greengrocery and debated his next move. As he pondered, a heavy-set woman shoved her way past him, nearly knocking him off his feet.

"I beg your pardon, ma'am," he said, as courteously as he could manage.

"Mind where you're going," she snapped back.

Another woman joined her. "Oh, it's him," she said loudly, and to Jacob, "What you doin' here?"

Jacob knew instinctively that the correct answer – "Buying carrots" – wouldn't be the sensible one.

"I apologize if I inconvenienced you," he said.

"Huh. That fancy talk don't fool me. Why don't you go back where you came from?"

"Do you mean Oxford?" Jacob asked, before he could stop himself.

"Oh, that's funny, that is," said the first woman. She raised a basket filled with purchases and swung it in Jacob's direction. She missed, but the momentum of the swing made her lose her balance, and she stumbled into him. Before Jacob could draw breath to comment or apologize, he found himself in the center of a minor melee, several women and youths shouting and pushing, and then pelting him with vegetables.

Someone yanked his coat and pulled it, throwing him off balance before he recovered his footing. It would have been almost amusing if he hadn't been hit with some heavier items and if he hadn't been worried the plant-based missiles would turn into something more lethal.

He had just decided he was going to have to abandon his usual policy of non-violence when a shrill whistle split the air, causing his attackers to pause and look around for the source.

Inspector Carey and Sergeant Bell were approaching at a trot, their faces grim. Bell clutched his whistle in one hand and was drawing out his truncheon with the other. Carey effortlessly stiff-armed someone foolish enough to try blocking his way and moved into the center of the group. A circle opened up around him.

"What's going on here?" the inspector demanded, as the crowd fell silent. Jacob brushed a couple of cabbage leaves off his coat and removed a sprout from his hat.

It seemed no one was going to answer, but finally a woman said, "The Jew attacked her," and pointed to the woman who had first shoved him.

Carey turned an inquisitive gaze on Jacob, who said calmly, "That's not true, Inspector."

"What happened, Mr Silver?"

"I believe she lost her balance and started to fall. Unfortunately, she stumbled into me as I stood outside the shop. I definitely did not assault her in any way."

Carey glared at the crowd, whose outer members were now trying to melt away unobtrusively. He raised his voice.

"I suggest all of you go about your business and refrain in future from making false accusations, causing an affray in a public place or assaulting an innocent citizen. If not, you may find yourselves in a great deal of trouble with the law."

"What's this about Mr Thomas Martyn?" someone called. "We reckon maybe he didn't die natural, not with a London inspector here lookin' into it."

Jacob gave his fellow citizens credit for working that out, despite their unnecessary aggression. He awaited Carey's reply with interest, noting that he had possibly been wrong about the inspector's air of authority. He had certainly defused the vegetable attack quickly enough.

"We have various people helping us with our inquiries and hope to resolve the matter soon," Carey said. "Now move along, please, before I change my mind about bringing any charges."

Jacob was intrigued and wondered if the first part of the statement could be true. When someone was described as helping the police with their inquiries, he knew it was frequently followed by their arrest. He settled his coat more firmly around his shoulders, thankful for his family's tailoring skills that had kept it from being pulled too far out of shape, and watched as the last of the vegetable throwers departed.

"You seem to have a gift for attracting trouble, Mr Silver," Carey said mildly.

"I did nothing," Jacob said. "One of the women deliberately pushed me, and although I apologized, the others joined in blaming me. Strength in numbers, I suppose, or an odd form of entertainment. Not to worry, Inspector, I'm used to it."

"I daresay."

"Although it's usually not quite as violent and I'm grateful for your intervention. The situation could have become rather ugly. May I ask, is there actually someone helping with your inquiries? Or was that merely to deflect the crowd's curiosity?"

"No, it's quite true, although somewhat premature," Carey said. "We haven't actually brought anyone in for questioning yet, but we will before the day is out."

"I see."

"You don't ask who it is, I note."

"I didn't think you would tell me or I would have done," Jacob said, allowing himself a smile. "Is it Jerome Mead?"

"That will become clear before the day is out, too, but I see no harm in telling you now. Mead was heard by several people, including yourself, to threaten Thomas Martyn, and he has no reliable alibi for the time of Martyn's death."

"So you will question him, and possibly arrest him?"

"If he cannot give us a better account of his whereabouts, yes. He denies any involvement, insists he was merely angry with Martyn, because of a personal matter which he refuses to divulge."

"I would think," Jacob said slowly, "under the circumstances, he would be wise to tell you what the matter was."

"I agree," Carey said.

"He's a troublemaker, that one," Bell muttered, and Jacob remembered Sarah describing Mead in much the same words.

"Have you found the weapon used?" he asked.

"No." The inspector sounded frustrated. "Dr Sheridan and our own surgeon both postulate a knife with a short, sharp blade, perhaps five or six inches in length, but such a knife can be found in every kitchen in Witney, I imagine, and could easily have been disposed of in the river."

He frowned in the general direction of the Windrush, as if it had no business providing a hiding place for a murder weapon. Jacob forbade from mentioning that it could be worse; the Windrush was a mere trickle compared to the Thames, if a search was required.

"Although you must be able to narrow it down to only a few kitchens," he said. "Are Mrs Mead or her cook missing a knife?"

"She says not," Carey said drily. "However, that is not exactly conclusive."

"Of course not. It may have been cleaned and returned to its place before anyone noticed its absence. Or it may not have come from a kitchen at all. Knives are used in many other places."

"Dr Sheridan was correct about you," Carey said. "Should you ever decide to abandon the clock repair trade, Mr Silver, you might consider a career as a detective. Together with your very intelligent housemaid you would make a formidable duo.

However, I should not be sharing this information with you in the first place. Why didn't you stop me, Sergeant?"

"Not my place, sir," Bell said.

Jacob felt it was time for him to make a tactical retreat.

"If I can be of any further help, please let me know," he said. "Thank you again for your assistance."

"That's quite all right," the inspector said. "And I expect we will speak again. I find you a curiously refreshing person. Good day, Mr Silver."

He touched his hat and walked away, Bell following him.

THIRTEEN

By the time Jacob arrived at his own house, he had stopped wondering about Carey's parting comment and was more concerned about the reaction of his domestic staff to his somewhat disheveled appearance.

He slipped quietly in the front door, listening. He could hear someone humming in the kitchen, and since Mrs Tucker didn't hum, he concluded she had left and Sarah was on her own. That suited him, since she undoubtedly would have something to say, but at least it wouldn't be repeated all over Witney.

He took off his coat and held it up for inspection, turning it around. The back had caught the worst of the missiles and there were streaks and spots of dirt and vegetable matter from the shoulders almost to the hem.

"Whatever have you been doin', Mr Silver?" Sarah asked from the kitchen doorway. "You've got stains and mud all over that good wool coat of yours. Did you fall?"

"I was involved in a bit of a fracas," Jacob said. He brushed his hat off and hung it up.

"A what, sir?"

"A fight."

Sarah's blue eyes widened. "A fight, sir? *You*?"

"I'm afraid so. And no, I didn't start it. Nor, as it happens, did I end it."

"You tell me who it was and I'll sort 'em out." Sarah was bristling with indignation and Jacob smiled.

"No, that's not necessary. Inspector Carey has already spoken to them."

"But what happened?"

Jacob briefly recounted the incident at the greengrocery, trying to make it sound more amusing than it had been, and moved on quickly to Carey's revelation that Jerome Mead was about to be questioned about Martyn's death. As expected, that was of more interest to Sarah than a few vegetable-throwing louts.

"Does that inspector think he did it?" she asked.

"I think it's more a case of not being able to identify anyone else who had a reason to want him dead. Mead threatened him, more than once, in the hearing of other people."

"I dunno," Sarah said. "I've heard about him, and he spouts off a lot, sayin' he's going to do this or that, but I reckon most of it's hot air. Can't really see him stickin' a knife into somebody."

"I doubt that will matter to the police. Of course, if they could find the knife that was used and connect it to Mead, they would have a much better case."

"Find one knife in all of Witney? Not a chance."

"Yes, that's what I think, too. It will have been well cleaned and either disposed of or put back wherever it came from."

"Oh, arr," Sarah said. "Reckon I'd better be gettin' that coat dried and brushed for you. Looks like mostly mud from them vegetables, so it'll come up all right."

"Thank you," Jacob said, handing her the coat.

"And there's some soup on the stove. Pity you didn't pick up some of what they was throwin' and then we could have had 'em for supper."

She whisked into the kitchen, Jacob's coat folded over her arm, and he smiled as he watched her go.

Jacob felt he had never been so glad when sunset arrived on Friday evening and he could light his Shabbat candles and officially put an end to his working week. Sarah had made a quick foray into town that afternoon and returned with the news that Jerome Mead had indeed been brought in to the police station for questioning, but in the absence of concrete evidence or anything resembling a prison, he had been released again and told to keep himself available.

That hadn't stopped the townspeople from deciding on the spot that he must have killed Thomas Martyn, a view apparently endorsed by the family. Nathaniel had been seen rubbing his hands together and heard to comment that the police had taken long enough to reach the obvious conclusion and he hoped the man would be locked up, sent to trial and then hanged without wasting any more time.

"And the funeral's tomorrow afternoon at two o'clock," Sarah reported. "Gracie says as how it's to be a very grand affair, with black horses and all. Can I go?"

"I thought the inspector warned you not to go to the Martyn house again," Jacob said.

"I didn't. Gracie was at the haberdasher's buying black ribbons and armbands for all the staff to wear. She gave me a ribbon." She held it up – a wide black grosgrain band that could be fastened around a hat to indicate mourning.

"I suppose there's no harm in you going to the funeral as long as you don't cause any problems."

"I know how to behave, Mr Silver. I could say it's on account of my ma having worked for them, if anybody asks."

"That's as good an excuse as any," Jacob said with a sigh. "It doesn't sound as though she left her position on particularly good terms with the Martyns, however."

"Dunno whether she did or not. She never talked about it much. You won't be there, will you, sir?"

"No, I won't be."

"I'll tell you if anything interesting happens."

Jacob couldn't imagine what might happen during a funeral that Sarah considered interesting, unless Jerome Mead made an appearance and was torn to pieces by a bloodthirsty mob. But he doubted Martyn had been popular enough to inspire that kind of loyalty. Most people outside of the immediate family would be attending the funeral service more out of curiosity or a desire to be seen, than to mourn.

On that thought, he tried to achieve mental as well as physical rest, but it was difficult when his thoughts kept returning to Martyn's death. Mead seemed almost too obvious a suspect, and why had he refused to tell Inspector Carey what the personal argument was about between himself and Martyn? It was ridiculous for Mead to risk being hanged when a simple explanation might clear him from suspicion. Unless it was not simple at all.

Normally, Jacob didn't see much of Sarah on Saturday or on Sunday morning, either. He kept to himself on Saturday, letting her go about her duties without his supervision, an arrangement which suited both of them. He discouraged her from cooking as well, and usually had only a simple cold meal. On Sunday morning, she went to church, an outwardly pious activity which Jacob suspected was undertaken as much for the social aspect as the spiritual one. While she was there, he busied himself in his workshop, so they usually didn't meet again until she returned and started to cook the Sunday dinner.

But this Saturday was obviously going to be different. Sarah moved about the kitchen like a small, determined whirlwind, preparing a plate of cold meat, pickle and bread for him to eat while she was out, and leaving the room spotless afterwards.

Then she disappeared up the stairs, coming back down a short while later wearing the best of her two dresses, a sober dark gray one. He caught a glimpse of polished boots under the hem. She put on her coat, buttoning it primly up to her chin, and settled her only hat on her head, the ends of the black ribbon trailing over the back of her collar.

"Do I look all right, Mr Silver? I've not been to a funeral since Ma's and Johnny's, and that weren't grand like this one. Just simple-like, in the church at Cogges, the one we always went to."

"You look very respectable, Sarah."

"S'pose no one will be looking at me, anyway."

"Probably not. But you appear suitably dressed for a funeral. Quite solemn and mournful."

She wrinkled her nose. "I expect it'll be mostly prayers, hymns and the vicar talkin' about what a good man he was. But I'll keep me eyes open, in case anything happens."

"Very well, although I doubt it will."

"I'd best start off now. They'll be lucky to get everyone in the church, big as it is. Standing room only, I reckon, maybe outside, even, for those of us not invited."

She went out the door and Jacob stood in the kitchen, thinking. There were several reasons why he wouldn't be attending Martyn's funeral, ranging from the religious to the practical. But Sarah's last comment had given him an idea.

He waited until she was out of sight, and then took his newly brushed coat from its hook. Sarah had done an excellent job of removing the mud and vegetable matter and he put it on, then settled his hat on his head. There was no prohibition against taking a relaxing walk on the Sabbath, so Jacob decided to do just that. If his walk happened to take him in the direction of St Mary's …

Ten minutes later, he was standing under the overhanging awning of the ironmonger's, which afforded him an excellent view of Church Green. He was just far enough away not to be noticed by most churchgoers, but close enough to monitor activity both on the green and at the church.

As the hands of the Buttercross clock moved toward two, Jacob found he had company in his watching post. A man had slipped in beside him and was grinning up at him.

"Come to watch the show, Silver? Don't blame you."

Josiah Morton was a rat of a man, small and thin, with a pointed nose, small eyes and slicked back hair. Jacob could almost see whiskers quivering when he spoke and always half expected to see a tail poking out from under his coat. He was cunning as a rat, too, but possessed of a surprisingly educated turn of speech. As one of the town's two pawnbrokers, his trade occasionally and regrettably overlapped with Jacob's, and they were acquaintances, if not friends.

"Curiosity, nothing more," Jacob said. "It promises to be quite an event. And you?"

"Oh, the same, the same. Look, there they go."

As they watched, a hearse drawn by four black horses moved slowly down the path from the Martyn house, followed on foot by Nathaniel and five other men whom Jacob assumed were relatives or close friends. As Sarah had predicted, the procession was lavish, the horses with black feather plumes on their bridles, and the hearse polished to a high sheen.

By squinting at its windows, Jacob could just make out the elaborate coffin inside, strewn with flowers. As one used to simple pine coffins, he found it garish and ostentatious, but he supposed the family wanted to make a statement concerning Martyn's importance and their own wealth. Certainly the visible male family members were expensively dressed, and he knew the women also would have spent a goodly amount of money on their extensive mourning wardrobe, which would be worn for months, if not years, after the funeral.

"Cost a fortune, that did," Morton said, appraising the hearse, the horses and the clothing with the eye of someone accustomed to quickly estimating values. "You can't say the family stinted on giving him a proper funeral."

Jacob nodded. "It's very impressive."

The hearse approached the church and drew to a halt. Morton, to Jacob's amazement, removed his hat and held it at chest height, bowing his head slightly as the pallbearers prepared to shoulder their burden.

"You think I'm not sincere in paying my respects to Thomas Martyn?" he asked, catching Jacob's skeptical sideways glance.

"I have no idea. I wouldn't have thought you were close."

"We weren't. I never met the man. It's my loss of business I'm grieving for."

Jacob's eyebrows shot upward and he said, "Surely Thomas Martyn had no need to pawn his belongings. He was a wealthy man, as far as I know."

"Oh, he was, he was," Morton agreed. "It's not *his* trade I'm losing."

Jacob thought this over and could only come up with one explanation.

"Someone else's, then? Such as his son?"

"They do say you're clever, Silver," Morton said, winking and replacing his hat. "Yes, that's it. Young Nathaniel is a steady customer of mine when he can't get his allowance from his pater to stretch from one month to the next. But now he'll be coming into money, won't he, so he'll have no more need of me."

The coffin was carried into the church and as far as Jacob was concerned, the show was over. As Sarah had said, prayers, hymns and eulogies would occupy the next hour, and he had no intention of standing outside, waiting for the mourners to emerge and follow the coffin to the churchyard for burial.

But Morton's remarks intrigued him. He wondered just how many people were aware of Nathaniel's financial state, and whether his father had been one of them. And that led him to contemplate if that had been the reason Martyn had given him the watch for safekeeping and Nathaniel had been so desperate to retrieve it. Had he run out of belongings to pawn and turned to a valuable family heirloom for ready cash? But in that case, why hadn't Martyn told him so? Embarrassment, or simply discretion?

"What sort of things did Nathaniel Martyn pawn?" he asked, aiming for a tone of casual inquiry.

"Jewelry, bric-a-brac, even a few small paintings," Morton said. "Anything he could get out of the house without being noticed, I reckon. Redeemed a few of them when he got his allowance or when he had a decent win at the gaming tables."

"So he gambles as well?"

"What else would he do? He isn't interested in the factory, isn't married, doesn't have a profession to practice. He goes up to London as often as he can, looking for entertainment, but the pater always drags him back. Pity, really. It's grand to be rich, but not if you're stuck in a little market town, bored to tears."

"Do you think he'll be forced to take more of an interest in the factory now?"

Morton shrugged. "Could be. Not my affair."

"Nor mine."

They watched as a few sheep, totally uninterested in human problems, nibbled at the grass on the green.

"I'd best be getting on," Jacob said. "I hope your trade isn't too badly affected by Martyn's death and Nathaniel's inheritance. Although I'm sure you have many other … customers."

"As do you," Morton said. "I've known a few things that went straight from your workshop to my cases."

"I know," Jacob said sadly.

Morton shot him a shrewd glance. "I heard tell a while back, something was nicked from you and you thought as it might come my way."

Jacob was instantly alert, wondering how much Morton knew of the matter.

"Yes, there was," he said, "but it seems it may not have been stolen at all, merely mislaid."

"Mislaid by you? Tell me another one."

"At any rate, it was returned without incident."

Morton nodded. He inclined his head toward the church. "Now that really *was* an incident. Have you had a visit from the high and mighty London police inspector?"

"We've spoken, yes."

"He came to see me this morning and asked me a few questions. A clever man, I think."

"I agree. I hope he is successful in his investigation."

"Do you?"

"Yes, I do," Jacob said firmly. "Good day, Morton."

"Good day, Silver."

Jacob was back at the house and innocently reading a book in the kitchen when Sarah returned from the funeral, full of suppressed excitement.

"Ever so grand it were, and Mr Martyn, he looked almost like himself. You wouldn't think to see him that he'd been stabbed to death and a tree dragged over him."

Jacob put a marker in his book and closed it. "How do you know that? Surely you didn't actually see him."

"No, Gracie told me. All the staff went to have a look at him laid out in the front room before they closed the coffin."

She seemed unaffected by this information, which made Jacob shudder and wonder if the viewing had been compulsory. It was one thing to bid a final farewell to a relative or close friend, but quite another when the deceased was an employer, and probably not one for whom the staff had any great affection.

"And the funeral, Mr Silver, it was like somethin' out of one of them London picture papers. The gentlemen all dressed up in their best, and the ladies' dresses – oh, they was lovely. Black, of course, but the very latest fashion and hats with veils and long black ribbons and feathers and all."

She surveyed her own modest hat, still sporting the black ribbon, with disapproval.

"Mrs Martyn was there, tryin' hard not to cry, and her daughter from Oxford, and Mr Martyn's sister, come all the way down from Birmingham. And lots of other people I don't know. Friends and relations, I expect."

"And Nathaniel?"

"Oh, arr. Don't know how sorry he was about his pa dying, but he did and said all the right things. I was real lucky, Mr Silver, to get a seat in a pew not far from the family. A bit squashed, it was, but I could see most everything."

Jacob was trying to think of a way to convey the information he had received from Morton without admitting he'd been in Church Green, when Sarah asked, "Could you see much from the ironmonger's?"

There was no point in denying it.

"Not as much as I'd have liked. How did you know I'd been there?"

"Oh, Mr Silver, nobody'd pass up the chance to see somethin' like that funeral. And you're always curious, just like me. Besides, I saw you over there just before I went into the church. I was looking, 'cause I thought you might be somewhere about, even though you said you wouldn't be."

"For once, I'm glad I gave in to my curiosity," Jacob said. "I had a very interesting conversation at the ironmonger's, and it was nothing to do with fashions."

Sarah settled herself on a chair, elbows propped on the table. Under the circumstances, Jacob didn't think he should comment.

"Who you been talkin' to, Mr Silver? When I looked, you was on your own."

Jacob gave her a quick summary of Morton's comments, adding, "He can't be dismissed just because his trade is a bit unsavory. He does provide a useful service."

"Oh, I know he does. Like those girls do."

"Slightly different, I would say, but I take your point. Anyway, the fact remains that Nathaniel benefits monetarily from his father's death, and if Morton is correct, he needs the inheritance to continue his lifestyle."

"The inspector will know that, too, sir, even if he don't know about him poppin' the things from the house."

"True. But I don't think he knows Nathaniel was so desperate that he brought a constable here, hoping to successfully accuse me of stealing his father's watch. Which beggars the question: How did Nathaniel know it was here?"

FOURTEEN

Even Sarah couldn't find an answer to that question, and Jacob certainly couldn't. He tried to keep his mind on subjects suited to Sabbath contemplation, but for once he was glad when the sun set and he could justify turning his thoughts back to the mystery of Martyn's death.

"There's something special about that watch," he said, and then was surprised to realize he'd spoken out loud.

"Too right," Sarah agreed. "Reckon it's worth a pretty penny."

Jacob decided not to remind her that was why she had stolen it in the first place.

"It's valuable, it's a beautiful example of the watchmaker's art, and it's a family heirloom," he said. "Put those three things together and it's easy to see why Thomas Martyn wanted it kept safe. He didn't want it to fall into the hands of a wayward son who would only see it as a means of financing his pleasures. I only wish he hadn't chosen me to give it to for safekeeping."

"Speakin' of pleasures," Sarah said, "I should have asked those girls if Mr Nathaniel was one of their punters. I was just thinkin' at the time of Mr Martyn, and why he'd be out in a storm. Didn't think of his son, but it seems kind of likely."

"I don't think it matters if he was," Jacob said. "From my meeting with him I should say he drinks to excess, Morton says he gambles and who knows what else he may indulge himself with. The point is that his father was determined he shouldn't use that watch to finance any of that."

"I wonder …" Sarah fell silent.

"What do you wonder?"

"Well, if Jerome Mead was threatenin' him, and it didn't have nothing to do with factory business, maybe it had somethin' to do with Mr Nathaniel. I mean, we know he said as you stole his pa's watch, and he said I stole some spoons, and neither of those were true. So maybe he lied about somethin' else – somethin' important and Mead caught him out and told Mr Martyn."

"And gave him an ultimatum," Jacob said. "That's possible, Sarah. Apparently he told Inspector Carey it was a personal matter, so it mightn't have anything to do with the factory."

"What's an ulti … what did you call it?"

"Ultimatum. A final demand. A threat, you might say. 'Either you do what I say, or else' sort of thing. Perhaps he told Martyn he had to stop Nathaniel from doing something, and for whatever reason, Martyn refused."

"Could be," Sarah said. "And if it was, then it was something worth killin' over."

After the events of Saturday, Sunday morning felt like something of an anticlimax. Mrs Tucker didn't come in on Sundays, and Sarah was up early, preparing Jacob's breakfast before setting off to church. He had never before thought to ask her which church she attended, but this time, before she went out the door, he did.

"Holy Trinity, up on Woodgreen," she said. "I know it's further to go, but St Mary's is for them with money, like the Martyns and such, and I don't want to go to Cogges. Makes me think of Ma and Johnny too much."

"I don't think anyone would mind if you went to St Mary's, since it's so much closer," Jacob said. "Isn't everyone supposed to be equal in the eyes of God?"

"Supposed to be, sir, but the looks us poor folk get there, you wouldn't think it. I don't mind walking to Woodgreen, 'cept when it's raining real hard."

"Very well. It's your choice, Sarah."

"Ta, Mr Silver. I'll be back in time to cook your dinner."

She went out and Jacob was left to contemplate why she preferred a half-hour's walk to a church on the other side of town, when she could have attended St Mary's, less than ten minutes away, or even the church at Cogges where her parents had worshipped and where she presumably had been christened and confirmed.

He would have accepted her explanations of social unsuitability and unpleasant associations, but somehow they didn't quite ring true. He pushed his skepticism to the back of his mind and went to his workshop for some uninterrupted time among the clocks and jewelry before she returned.

His workshop window looked out onto Corn Street, which gave Jacob a view of his neighbors walking to church and casting disapproving eyes at his house as they passed. After five years in Witney he was used to it, but it still stung that they couldn't afford his faith the same respect he gave theirs. With a sigh, he turned back to examine an elegant ladies' watch which its owner had described as 'broken', but which turned out merely needing to be cleaned and freshly oiled.

The way the tiny toothed wheels inside the watch meshed together reminded Jacob of society in general. One wheel turned another, which pushed a third, and so on, until the desired result was obtained. A police investigation was much the same, he supposed, one fact leading to and meshing with another until the criminal was correctly identified.

Of course, with an investigation, all sorts of odd facts which might be totally irrelevant could interfere with the process, like bits of grit keeping the wheels from turning as they should.

Pleased with his analogy, he bent over the watch again, giving it a final polish before putting it away to deliver to its owner. He rubbed his eyes and stretched, easing his cramped shoulder and neck muscles.

Then on an impulse, he took Thomas Martyn's watch out of the drawer, first looking through the window to make sure no one was looking in. He turned the watch one way and then another, opened the lid and examined it closely, finding no hidden contents or cryptic messages. It was just what it seemed to be – a beautiful, valuable heirloom. And practical as well, since he had cleaned it and set it to functioning properly.

Inside the lid was the engraving, the initials TGM and the date 1815. Jacob did some mental arithmetic and deduced that since Thomas Martyn had been in his mid-fifties, he must have been born shortly before his father went off to war. That in turn meant that the elder Martyn already knew he had a son who would inherit, and must have been pleased when his own father had presented him with the watch on his return.

He wondered briefly what had prompted Martyn's father to be at Waterloo in the first place. Soldiering was obviously not a family tradition, so perhaps his presence with Wellington's troops had been for a more mundane purpose, such as supplying saddle blankets.

Or it was possible that a patriotic impulse had prompted him to help fight the French, and he actually had taken part in the decisive battle. In that case, Thomas Martyn's grandfather must have been doubly delighted to see his son return safely, so that he could eventually take over the family business.

Jacob felt the familiar pang of loss at this, knowing that unless he took some positive action, there would be no one to inherit from him. His older brother and sister both had children, but nieces and nephews weren't quite the same. However, he thought wryly, having no heirs was probably preferable to having one like Nathaniel Martyn.

On that thought, he returned the watch to the drawer, locked it, slid off his stool and went into the kitchen. Judging from previous Sundays, Sarah would be back before long and would get to work preparing their Sunday dinner.

He had boiled the kettle and just settled down to a cup of tea when the scullery door flew open and Sarah came in. She was breathless, and he hoped she hadn't run all the way from Woodgreen, a distance of a mile or so.

"Here, sit down," he said. "I've just made a pot of tea – do you want a cup?"

"In a minute," she panted. "Need to catch my breath first. Oh, Mr Silver, do you know what's just happened?"

"No. I've been here, working."

"That inspector, he's arrested Jerome Mead for murderin' Mr Martyn."

Jacob was surprised, given Carey's uncertainty about Mead's guilt on Friday afternoon. Unless some more evidence had come to light in the interim.

"I wonder what made him do that. He must have discovered something new."

"Dunno. But wasn't it lucky I just happened to be passin' by at the time? I've never seen anybody arrested before. Mead was shouting and swearing and saying he hadn't done nothing to Mr Martyn. But the inspector wasn't payin' him no mind. The sergeant was kind of holdin' him still so the inspector could fasten his wrists together, and then he and the sergeant took him away. Down the High Street in broad daylight, they did."

Sarah's face was glowing with excitement and she clearly wanted to share the experience, so Jacob obliged her.

"Where did they arrest him, Sarah? In the High Street?"

"No, at his house. Mead lives down by the factory, just off Bridge Street. I was walkin' past on my way back from church."

"I trust you actually went to church first."

"You don't believe me, do you, sir?" Sarah sounded offended and Jacob felt guilty, but only for a moment. He reminded himself of her tendency to manipulate the truth and disregarded the wide blue eyes that gazed at him.

"Did you?"

"Oh, arr. Then when I was comin' back I heard all the commotion, so I went to see what it was about."

It sounded believable enough, and Jacob supposed Sunday wasn't a day of rest for the police when a murder was involved.

"All right, Sarah, I believe you. A cup of tea?"

"Ta." Sarah went to hang up her shawl and returned to the table. "Do you suppose he really did kill Mr Martyn?"

"I don't know. Presumably the inspector thinks he did, so he must have found some evidence."

"Like the knife?"

"Yes, but I don't know how they'd prove it was the one which killed Martyn. There must be something else."

They drank their tea in pensive silence and then Sarah said, "I'd best get the dinner started, sir."

She stood up and began to assemble the ingredients for the meal while Jacob sat at the table, lost in thought. Finally he said, "Sarah, you said you saw Mead being taken away by the police. Taken to where, do you know?"

"There's no prison here in Witney, so they was going to keep him locked up at the police station 'til they could take him to Oxford and the prison there."

She shot Jacob a sideways glance. "I was close enough to hear the inspector sayin' that to the sergeant, in case you was wondering, before they went off."

Jacob tried not to visualize Sarah and whoever else had been passing, edging as close as possible to milk the most information and excitement from the unusual event.

"And you said you heard Mead shouting and swearing?"

"Yes."

"Shouting and swearing what? Could you hear what he said, or was that before you got close enough to eavesdrop?"

Sarah turned from the stove, where she was wrestling a plucked and drawn pheasant into a roasting pan.

"Not too much of it, sir, but I did hear one or two things."

"Which were?"

"Like I said, he kept shouting that he hadn't touched Mr Martyn, hadn't done a thing to him and that they had the wrong man."

"And what did the inspector say to that?"

Sarah frowned. "Only that he – Mead, that is – had some explainin' to do. I guess he was refusin' to say where he'd been that night, so maybe it was somewhere he oughtn't to have been."

She deftly balanced the roasting pan on the rack over the fire and turned to the vegetables that would accompany it.

"Quite likely. Anything else?"

"He said something else after he'd quietened down a bit, just before they marched him off. He said he reckoned it – Mr Martyn bein' killed, I guess he meant – was because of the girl."

"What girl?" Jacob asked, startled. "There's no girl involved in this, is there?"

"Not that I know of, sir, but that's what he said."

"How very strange. I wonder what he meant. Did other people hear him say that?"

"Reckon so. There was a few of us watchin'."

"So he must have known all of you would hear him. That makes it even odder. If the girl – whoever she is – was providing an alibi for him, or something of that nature, you'd think he would have told the inspector in confidence, not said it where anyone could hear."

"You would do, sir. Or maybe the girl was the one what killed Mr Martyn and Mead knew about it."

Jacob felt his head was whirling. The whole mystery of Martyn's death was puzzling enough without some unidentified girl now being involved in it. He suspected Sarah felt the same, since she was peeling and chopping carrots as if she had Mead under her knife and was about to force a confession from him.

"And nobody knew what he meant; who the girl was?" He took it for granted that the spectators would have consulted each other.

"No, sir, they didn't."

"She wouldn't possibly be one of the prostitutes you spoke to, would she?"

"Don't think so, sir. They mostly keep to this end of town, 'round Church Green and such, where the rich punters are."

"But this end of town is where Martyn was killed. I know they said he wasn't a customer of theirs, but would Mead have been?"

"Dunno. I can go back and ask them, if you want."

"No, no, you've done enough. I don't want you wandering the streets in the middle of the night, asking questions of prostitutes."

"I can take care of myself, sir."

"I'm quite aware of that, Sarah. But some people may, shall we say, misinterpret what you're doing there."

"Ah, I see what you mean." Sarah thought for a moment. "Fred could go. Nobody would pay him any mind."

"No, he couldn't," Jacob said sternly. "Let Inspector Carey do his job. That's what he's come here for. If he wants any help from either of us, he knows where to find us."

Jacob expected that Mead's arrest would be the talk of the town by the end of the day, and he was correct. Sunday might be a day outwardly devoted to spiritual, character-improving activities, but like the woolen mills, gossip never rested.

Servants still had their work to do after compulsory church attendance, and when he took a walk after his excellent dinner of roast pheasant, potatoes and carrots, he caught glimpses of furtive conversations taking place at back doors and quiet alleys, no doubt sharing the news.

He went as far as Church Green, taking care to avoid the devout churchgoers leaving St Mary's after the late service, and strolled past the police station. He failed to see Jerome Mead peering from a window, so assumed he was being detained in a back room. He also failed to see Inspector Carey or either of the two local officers. Either they were guarding their prisoner or were occupied elsewhere.

He crossed the green far enough down to avoid emerging in front of the Martyn house, since he hardly expected to be welcomed, and wanted to avoid the embarrassment of being chased off by the butler like one of the twig-snipping lads.

Lights were showing behind the black coverings over the front windows, and Jacob could imagine the conversations going on inside. He had never met Evangeline Martyn or her daughter Charlotte, but he fervently hoped one or both of them had the backbone to stand up to Nathaniel, who was no doubt glorying in his new status as head of the family.

The night was drawing in and it was starting to rain, so he walked back along the end of the green and turned his steps down Corn Street toward his own house.

Perhaps because of the unusual activities of Saturday and Sunday, Jacob found it hard to fall sleep. Thoughts and theories chased themselves around his mind, no matter how many times he firmly reminded himself that Martyn's death and the subsequent investigation were none of his business. None of his business, that was, unless someone like Inspector Carey came hammering at his front door, demanding to know why he was hiding an expensive watch belonging to a murdered man.

He finally fell into a restless sleep just as the first cockerels began to crow.

Downstairs in the kitchen, Sarah crept around as quietly as possible, stirring up the fire and setting the kettle to boil for morning tea. Jacob heard none of this, since he was sound asleep, dreaming of being pursued by large numbers of police officers.

They were blowing whistles and armed with truncheons, and they were all intent on clapping handcuffs onto Jacob and arresting him for some undisclosed crime. His house failed to offer any sanctuary, since the officers were streaming through the scullery door, shouting.

Jacob awoke with a start, realizing it was much later than the time he usually rose, but puzzled as to why the voices of the officers were still audible, although higher pitched than he would have expected.

He sat up in bed, listening. There was a great deal of noise coming from his kitchen, the clatter of pots and pans and two female voices raised in excited conversation. Jacob swung his legs out from under the blanket and went to stand in the doorway, where he could make out distinct words.

"And so I says to Mattie, if this goes on, I shan't feel safe goin' anywhere anymore." It was Mrs Tucker, more agitated than Jacob had ever heard her, even during her numerous complaints about Sarah. "It might have been me, lyin' there."

"You're right, you know, none of us'll be safe," Sarah agreed. "Just wait 'til Mr Silver hears about this."

Jacob scrambled into his clothes, splashed some water on his face and went downstairs.

"I'm sorry I overslept," he said. "Good morning, Sarah, Mrs Tucker. I gather something momentous has happened?"

"If that means horrible, arr, it has," Mrs Tucker said. "We'll all be murdered in our beds, next thing we know."

"But what …"

Sarah interrupted as Mrs Tucker drew breath to start another complaint about her personal safety.

"There's been another one," she told Jacob. "Mrs Tucker says a dead body was found by the river under the bridge, down by the factory. A girl."

FIFTEEN

By using a combination of coaxing, questioning and flattery, and aided by several cups of tea, Jacob and Sarah managed to persuade Mrs Tucker to reveal all the information she possessed about the girl whose body had been found. Stripped of adjectives and speculation, it wasn't very much.

Mrs Tucker lived in a cottage on the edge of town, and she usually took a shortcut along the riverbank to walk to Jacob's house, especially if it was raining. This morning it had been drizzling – "fair spitting, it was" – so she had gone that way.

As she hurried along the path, she became aware of a clump of people standing on the bank by the old stone bridge that spanned the Windrush, a few hundred yards from the blanket factory. Some of them were kneeling on the ground by a huddled form, and when Mrs Tucker got a little closer, she could see that it was a girl, fully dressed but undeniably dead.

"Her face was all white, not a drop of color in it," she explained, while Sarah made soothing noises and refilled the tea cup. "Fair turned my stomach, seeing the poor soul like that."

"That must have been very upsetting for you, Mrs Tucker," Jacob said, trying to sound sympathetic. It wasn't easy, since she was clearly relishing the experience. "Had she drowned in the river, then?"

"You'd think so, Mr Silver, but maybe not, as they was sayin' there was a lot of blood on her dress."

"Where?" Sarah asked.

"On her dress, as I said."

"I mean, what part of her dress? The skirt, the sleeves?"

"No, on the …" Mrs Tucker darted an embarrassed glance at Jacob.

"Bodice?" he suggested.

"Arr. Soaked with blood, they said. And it was torn, like."

Jacob and Sarah exchanged glances. "Was she found in the river, do you know?" Jacob asked Mrs Tucker. "Or on the bank beside it?"

"Dunno, sir. Think she was on the bank, as it was a lad fishing who found her. He said she was hidden, nearly, under some bushes and under the bridge."

In the absence of convenient fallen tree branches, Jacob thought, and then wondered why he had instantly assumed the two deaths were the handiwork of the same person.

"So the boy went to fetch the constable?"

"Oh, arr. He was just coming when I passed by, and when he'd had a look, he chased everyone off, so we didn't find out anything else."

She sounded aggrieved, but Jacob silently applauded the constable for clearing the curious onlookers from what could well be another murder scene. He supposed Dr Sheridan had also been summoned, as soon as the constable realized the girl had not died of any natural cause.

"Did they know who she was?" Sarah asked. Jacob doubted that anyone did, since that would have been the first item of news to share, if known.

"Well, *I* didn't know her," Mrs Tucker said. She added grudgingly, "Course I don't know everybody in Witney. And nobody else seemed to, either. Constable said he'd be asking around. Poor thing."

"No doubt he will be able to identify her and her family – if she has one – will be notified," Jacob said. He looked at Sarah, who shrugged slightly, conveying her opinion that Mrs Tucker probably didn't have anything else helpful to contribute.

"Thank you for telling us, Mrs Tucker," he said. "I know it must have been a dreadful experience for you. But sad as it is, I think we should carry on with the day's work now."

"You haven't had your breakfast yet," Sarah pointed out.

"I'm not very hungry, but I'll take a piece of bread and butter and my tea to the workshop."

He knew Sarah would use his absence to extract any more information from Mrs Tucker, but he felt sure the dead girl was the same one Mead had mentioned. What she had to do with Mead or Thomas Martyn and why she had died, however, was something he couldn't begin to speculate about. He pushed the thought to one side and got to work.

Monday was normally washing day, which meant that Mrs Tucker would be there at least until midday to deal with sheets and other large or heavy items, leaving Sarah to finish up the lighter laundry in the afternoon on her own. The pattern was followed today, and eventually Sarah tapped lightly on the workshop door.

"There's a bit of cold pheasant left from yesterday for your dinner, Mr Silver," she said, "and Mrs Tucker's just leavin'."

"Thank you, Sarah. I'll be there in a minute."

He waited a good five minutes, until he heard the scullery door close, then went into the kitchen, where damp sheets hung from the overhead drying racks. Jacob dodged between them with the ease of long practice and sat at the table. Sarah placed the plate of cold meat and bread in front of him.

"I thought Mrs Tucker'd never go," she said. "Made that news last a long time, she did. Mr Silver, I reckon that poor girl that died is the one Mead was talkin' about when they arrested him, don't you?"

"Quite likely."

"And it sounds like she was stabbed to death, just like Mr Martyn was."

"Yes, it does, if there was a great deal of blood on the bodice of her dress. But without a convenient fallen branch to cover the wound and mislead observers this time. I wonder if Dr Sheridan will be able to tell when she died. Even if he can't be precise …"

Sarah easily followed his reasoning to the next step.

"'Cause if it was last night or early this morning," she said, "then it weren't Jerome Mead who killed her, being as he was locked up in the police station."

A second violent death within a week might not have been an unheard event for Witney, but it gave the citizenry plenty to talk about. Accordingly, Sarah was dispatched to the market and returned an hour later with a basketful of vegetables, a piece of fish and all the latest gossip.

The dead girl's name was Sally Wright. She was fifteen years old and had worked on the looms at Martyn's factory, a fact which set numerous tongues wagging as they tried to connect her place of employment with her late employer's death. She was an orphan, lodging with an aunt and trying to make her way in the world, a difficult task for a girl with minimal education and no family support to speak of.

A few people had come forward to give her a posthumous character reference, describing her as a quiet girl who had worked hard and never caused any trouble to anyone. She had no known enemies, or even anyone who disliked her.

"Nothing special about her," was the communal verdict. "No reason for anyone to want to do her harm."

A young man who worked on a nearby farm had been courting her, but was instantly dismissed from suspicion on the grounds that he had been within sight and sound of other people – and a mile away – during the crucial period. He was reported to be devastated by the news of her death and as mystified as anyone else as to how she had ended up being brutally murdered and her body left half hidden under a bridge in the center of the town.

The constable had not been able or willing to contribute any information beyond what the onlookers had already seen. There had been a great deal of blood on the front of the girl's dress and on the ground beside her, so it appeared that she had been stabbed in the chest and had bled to death. No weapon had been found.

At the moment, it seemed, Sally Wright was at Dr Sheridan's surgery, where she had been transported by the constable and a reluctant assistant plucked from the crowd of onlookers, once the doctor and Carey had seen her *in situ*.

Sarah also reported that Jerome Mead was still being held at the police station, now helping with inquiries into two deaths, although Carey apparently had come to the same conclusion Jacob and Sarah had. A man being held under guard in a police station cannot commit a murder half a mile away from it at the same time.

The question, of course, was whether the two deaths were connected, even if not committed by the same person, and like Carey, the same crowd which had been baying for Mead's blood the previous day was now having second thoughts.

As unpopular as the man had been in some quarters, even his worst detractors found it hard to believe he could have escaped from the police station, stabbed an innocent girl and returned to the station, all without being noticed by the constabulary or anyone else.

Jacob was as puzzled as anyone, or perhaps more, and although Sarah was a reliable source of information, he knew she liked to embroider the basic facts a bit to make them more exciting. So, for example, he doubted that Mead had shouted and sworn too vehemently as he was being arrested. Protested, perhaps, but violent resistance would only have made the situation worse, even for one reputed to have a hot temper.

He was still thinking about this when he heard a tentative knock on the scullery door. Sarah had completed her intelligence-gathering report and gone upstairs to brush the carpet with the damp tea leaves from breakfast, so Jacob opened it, to find the same urchin who had previously summoned him to Sheridan's surgery.

"Doctor wants to know if you c'n come and see him," he said. "Soon as you can, he says."

Jacob frowned. "Did he say why?"

The boy shook his head.

"Very well. I'll come as soon as possible." Jacob fished in his pocket for two pennies and gave them to the boy, who muttered, "Ta, mister", and scampered off down the lane behind the house.

Jacob went into the hallway and called up the stairs to Sarah. She was on her knees on the carpet, wielding the brush, and looked up at the sound of his voice.

"Sir?"

"I'm going into town for a short while. It seems Dr Sheridan wants to see me about something. And no, I don't know what it may be."

"Reckon it has something to do with Mr Martyn, sir?"

"I've no idea. For all I know, he has a clock needing to be repaired."

He took his coat and hat and walked as quickly as possible to the Market Square surgery. As before, Sheridan's housekeeper-cum-nurse opened the door to him, but not before Jacob had observed the undertaker's vehicle waiting on the street outside. He braced himself as he walked down the corridor to the indicated room. A small form covered by a white sheet lay on the examining table, and Sheridan stood beside it.

"Thank you for coming, Silver," he said. "I know this isn't pleasant, but I have observed something and I want to see if you agree with me."

"I'm not a medical man, doctor."

"I know that. But you're an intelligent one. And there is another reason, which I will tell you in a moment. But first, if you are willing, I'd like to you look briefly at the unfortunate girl found by the river this morning, before the undertaker takes her away."

Jacob drew a deep breath and looked at the face revealed when Sheridan pulled the sheet back. Sally Wright was young, her face unmarked, her light brown hair now dull. She might have been attractive, or even pretty, while alive, but with all the vitality drained from her features, it was hard now to imagine what her personality might have been like.

Jacob had assumed the doctor wanted him for some reason to see the stab wound in her chest, and steeled himself to look at it, but Sheridan simply covered the girl's face again before turning to address him.

"Sally Wright was fifteen years old. She was approximately five feet tall, slight build, light brown hair, blue eyes. Nothing remarkable or unusual about her features. I have learned she was an orphan, and would have been in the workhouse – or worse – had her aunt not taken her in and helped her find employment at the Martyns' factory."

Jacob felt a slight shiver crawl down his spine.

"Do you draw the same conclusion I do, Silver?"

"Possibly."

"And that is?"

"The girl's age, appearance, her circumstances and even her name are very similar to those of my housemaid, since Sally is usually a diminutive of Sarah. Are you saying, sir, that you believe someone killed an innocent girl, mistakenly thinking she was Sarah Simm?"

SIXTEEN

"I don't know," Sheridan said bluntly. "But yes, that notion occurred to me, and I felt I owed it to you as her employer to share my observations. How much do you know about Sarah Simm?"

"Her background, do you mean?"

"Yes."

"Not very much," Jacob admitted. "But I know she is an orphan and was living in the Razor Hill workhouse before I employed her. Her father died three years ago, I believe she said, and her mother and younger brother last winter. She has never mentioned any other relations."

"And she has had several brushes with the law in the past year or so," Sheridan said. "I know about those, so there's no reason to prevaricate."

"Of course not. I wouldn't have denied it. But she works hard, and since she has been with me, she has given me no cause to doubt her honesty."

He felt he might be stretching the truth a bit with that statement, but he was certain Sarah had not reverted to theft since she'd come to live in his household. She was guilty of gossip, a few small falsehoods, self-inflicted injury and impersonating an errand boy, but not theft.

"And has she any enemies?"

"Not that I know of."

"She's never spoken of anyone wanting to do her harm?"

"No, sir, not at all." Jacob allowed himself a faint smile. "I am usually the one who is the target of any abuse, verbal or physical."

"So I've heard," Sheridan said drily. "But I also mention this matter because Miss Simm seems to regard you as somewhat more than an employer."

Jacob's eyebrows shot up. "I hope you're not suggesting any impropriety, sir, because there is none."

"Not as such. However, I understand it is only the two of you living in the house and she displays a lack of respect which I personally would find … disconcerting … in a housemaid. There is a certain amount of gossip, as I am sure you can appreciate."

"Gossip doesn't bother me," Jacob said. "I've faced far worse. But thank you for telling me. As for Sarah, I would rather employ a housemaid who is intelligent and cheerful than a po-faced one, even if she is a bit too familiar with me on occasion. She's high-spirited, nothing more."

"That, of course, is your decision," Sheridan said, with the air of one who had delivered his opinion and was now washing his hands of the matter. Jacob wondered who the gossipmongers were, and then decided there were probably too many to identify individually. Meanwhile, there was a more serious matter at hand. He looked back at the small body on the doctor's table.

"Doctor, were you able to ascertain when Miss Wright died?" he asked.

"Not precisely, but she had been dead for several hours before the boy discovered her body. I would say up to eight hours earlier, or somewhere around nine or ten o'clock last night."

There was a discreet tap on the door and Sheridan said, "Come."

The undertaker stood in the doorway, a second man behind him. "Are you ready for us, doctor?"

"Yes, I believe so." He looked at Jacob, who nodded.

They both stood silently as the undertaker and his assistant removed Sally Wright's body, loading it onto a stretcher with surprising gentleness and carrying it out.

When the door had closed behind them, Sheridan said, "This must be resolved, Silver. I may be mistaken, and in a way I hope I am, but if not …"

"Have you spoken to Inspector Carey about your suspicion?"

"Suspicion may be too strong a word. It was simply an idea that struck me as I examined the girl, but the fact is that you noticed it as well. And no, I haven't spoken to Inspector Carey yet, since his purpose here is to investigate Thomas Martyn's death, not Sally Wright's."

"And if the two deaths are somehow connected?"

"If so, he will need to widen the scope of his investigation."

"Yes," Jacob said slowly. "He will need to. Jerome Mead may or may not have been responsible for Thomas Martyn's death, but he did not kill Sally Wright."

Jacob was torn as to whether to share Sheridan's theory with Sarah. He didn't want to frighten her – not that she seemed to frighten easily – but he also wanted her to be more careful than she sometimes appeared to be. A girl who would fake a theft and then fling herself onto cobblestones merely to obtain some information was not one who could be trusted to take necessary precautions. And one who would sneak out before dawn to question prostitutes might be unwittingly putting herself in real danger from any number of sources.

In the end, he felt he had to warn her, so when he returned to the house he called her to the kitchen. He repeated Sheridan's suspicion and watched her eyes widen, not with fright, but in indignation.

"I don't believe it … Mr Silver, that's horrible, if he's right. The poor girl."

"Yes, indeed it is, but it's too late to do anything about Sally Wright's fate, except perhaps to help the police find out who killed her. I'm far more concerned about your safety."

"I can look after myself, sir."

"No doubt Sally thought the same thing. Dr Sheridan thinks she died at about nine or ten o'clock last night. I suppose she was walking home in the dark after working at the factory, taking the shortest route along the river and minding her own business, when she was attacked."

"But she weren't expecting it, and with all respect to that Sally, she might not be as good at fightin' off people as me."

Jacob frowned at her. Like the late Sally Wright, she was about five feet tall and probably weighed no more than seven stone. "Who did you fight off, Sarah?"

She looked down at the table and said, "Some people at the workhouse. Called me names, they did, so I took care of 'em."

"I'm sorry to hear that," Jacob said, meaning it sincerely. As he had told Sheridan, he knew all too well what it was like to be the target of abuse. "But this isn't a fistfight, it's someone with a knife, out to kill. I don't want to sound melodramatic, Sarah, but please think back and tell me. Is there anyone from the workhouse, or anywhere else, who went beyond name calling? Someone who might have a reason to want you dead?"

He half expected her to snap back a negative answer or accuse him of exaggerating the danger, but she took the question seriously, propping her elbows on the table and resting her chin in her cupped hands. Sheridan's words about lack of respect flashed through Jacob's mind as he watched her, thinking a better-trained housemaid would never sit like that in her employer's presence. She probably wouldn't sit at all, for that matter.

After a minute or so, she shook her head.

"Don't think so. Like I said, it was just name-calling and the like. Nothing to get wound up about. A few punches and hair-pulling and so on and it was over."

"What about those times before you came here when you stole things from market stalls? I can't see that would incite anyone to murder, but you must have made the stallholders angry."

"Suppose so, sir, but that was a long time ago."

"It's been only a few weeks, Sarah."

"Still. And like you say, they might have been cross, but none of 'em would follow me down to the river at night and stab me over a bun or two gone missing."

"No, probably not," he agreed.

"Is Dr Sheridan going to tell that inspector about what he thinks?"

"I don't know, but I imagine so. If he's wrong, then no harm done."

"And if he's right?"

Their eyes met and Jacob said, "Then you are going to be extremely cautious until this person is caught. I suppose you will be safe enough going to the market, but nowhere else. Don't even go to gossip with Gracie. Don't go anywhere if there aren't other people around, and do *not* go out after dark or before daybreak. If you are here in the house by yourself, do not answer the door to anyone whom you don't know personally. If I am not here and a message arrives purporting to be from me, ignore it. Do you understand me, Sarah?"

He had spoken more severely than he intended, and hoped she wouldn't storm off saying she could look after herself. But she sat silently as if reviewing his list of orders, and finally said, "I understand, sir."

"I'm only concerned for your safety."

"I know that." She smiled, a little shakily. "Ta, Mr Silver."

Jacob was correct in thinking Dr Sheridan would decide not to keep his mistaken identity theory to himself, and would communicate it to Inspector Carey before the day was out. He learned this when he heard firm footsteps coming up to his door, and looked out to see the inspector approaching with Bell, like a faithful shadow, a pace or two behind him.

He went to let them in, knowing Sarah could hear what was said in the hallway.

"Good afternoon, Inspector."

"Good afternoon, Mr Silver. I expect you know why I'm here."

"Yes, I do, if you've been speaking to Dr Sheridan."

"I have been. It's a very disturbing theory."

"It certainly is. I assume you are thinking I may be able to help you prove or disprove it."

"If not yourself, then Miss Simm. Is she aware of the doctor's suspicions?"

"Yes, she is. I thought she should know. And she can think of no reason why anyone would want to harm her."

"Nevertheless, I should like to speak with her. Is she present?"

"Yes, sir." Jacob went to the kitchen door. "Sarah, Inspector Carey wishes to speak with you. The parlor would be best, I think."

"Yes, Mr Silver." Sarah came into the hallway and bobbed her head in greeting to the two officers, who regarded her gravely. They all moved into the parlor and sat down, the three men forming a semi-circle with Sarah facing them.

"Miss Simm, I understand that Mr Silver has told you of Dr Sheridan's theory. His idea," he added, as if Sarah would need the word defined.

"I know what he means," Sarah said, an edge to her tone. "The doctor thinks somebody thought they was stabbin' me to death, but instead it was that poor Sally."

Carey looked at Jacob and saw no help there. He turned back to Sarah. "Yes, that's about the size of it. So you understand why I need to ask you some questions."

"Yes, sir."

"Did you know Sally Wright?"

"Never seen nor heard of her, sir."

"You're certain of that? You were about the same age."

"Doesn't mean I knew her, sir. I didn't."

"Very well. You're a bright girl, so you understand that if the person who attacked her thought she was you, he or she must have had a reason to think you'd be walking along that footpath late at night. Why would they think that?"

Sarah lifted her chin and looked straight at Carey.

"I don't know, sir."

"You don't ever walk along that footpath, especially after dark?"

"No, sir. No reason to. Can I say something?"

"Of course."

"Maybe it weren't the place so much as the girl. I mean, he might have been following her, like, for a long way, waitin' for a chance to get her alone, and the path down by the river was the first place he got it."

Before Carey could respond, she added, "If you was goin' to kill somebody, sir, and not get caught for it, you'd have to have a good place to leave 'em so nobody would find 'em for a while, wouldn't you? Give you a chance to get clean away. So that path was perfect."

Carey stared at her and then said, "An excellent observation. You may well be correct."

"Thank you, sir."

"I know Mr Silver has asked you, but I will ask again, officially: Have you any enemies, anyone who would want to harm you? Please be honest."

"Not that I know of, sir. That's the honest truth."

"Are you acquainted with a man called Jerome Mead?"

The question caught Jacob by surprise. Sarah merely said, "Not acquainted, sir. I know who he is, 'cause I knew some girls who worked in the blanket factory and they talked about him sometimes."

"So you have no personal connection to him?"

"No, sir."

"Have you ever worked at the factory?"

"No, sir."

"What did your acquaintances say about Mr Mead?"

Sarah's mouth twitched. "They didn't like him much, sir. Said he was a troublemaker."

"Did they mention anything specific?"

"They said as he was always tryin' to organize them, sayin' they could get more money that way. But they didn't want to, 'cause what would have happened would be they'd be out the door and have no money at all. Mr Martyn ain't generous, even though I guess he thought he was."

"Thomas Martyn, you mean?"

"Yes, sir."

"Did the girls say they were treated well at the factory?"

To Jacob's surprise, Sarah didn't answer immediately. It was as if she was trying to frame an answer that would be honest, yet leave out some vital item. And it surprised him even more to realize he knew her well enough to recognize this. Carey, who didn't, waited for her to respond.

"Most of the time, sir," she said finally.

"But not all the time?"

Sarah didn't answer and Jacob said, "Sarah, if you know anything that might help find who killed Sally Wright, please tell the inspector. It won't go any further."

She shot him a look that said as clearly as words, *I don't want to tell him*, but after a moment, she said, "There was a time or two when they weren't. Course it depends on how you look at it."

"Can you tell me what happened? I know you didn't work there, so I appreciate it won't be a first-hand account."

Sarah still hesitated. "It don't – doesn't – have nothin' to do with Sally Wright, least I don't think it does."

"Suppose you let me decide that," Carey said, with what Jacob assumed was intended as a reassuring smile.

"Don't let on as I told you. Please, sir."

"I won't. It will be information received from an anonymous source."

Sarah darted a questioning look at Jacob, who nodded.

"All right. There was a girl who lost her job there 'cause she … got into trouble."

"In what way?"

"A baby," Sarah said, obviously surprised that she needed to explain. "She had a baby and she weren't married. The baby died and she wanted her job back and he wouldn't let her."

"Who wouldn't let her come back? Jerome Mead? Surely that wouldn't be his decision to take."

"No, no, he was tryin' to help her. Said bygones was bygones and she'd suffered enough and why couldn't she go back? It was Thomas Martyn what wouldn't let her. Said she was a fallen woman, or some such nonsense."

Jacob remembered Martyn saying that all he required from his employees was diligence, honesty and respectability. Giving birth to an illegitimate child, even if the child had died, clearly disqualified this particular employee.

"And was the girl in question Sally Wright?" Carey asked.

"No, 'cause she was still workin' there, wasn't she?"

"So she was," Carey said. He sounded faintly irritated at having been caught out. "When did this incident happen, do you know?"

"Why, just now, sir, a few weeks ago, that is. She was at the workhouse when I left 'cause she didn't have nowhere else to go and her people didn't want her after what happened, but she said as how she was hopin' to go up north somewhere or maybe to London. Make a new start where nobody would know her and ask questions. I don't know if she's still there."

And she, not Sally Wright, must be the girl Mead was referring to, Jacob thought. *The one he threatened Martyn about. What a tangled web this has become. But why would …*

Aloud, he said, "Sarah, did you know the girl who lost her job?"

"Not very well, sir."

"Well enough that she might have said who the child's father was?"

Sarah looked shocked. "Oh, no, sir, she never told me. Don't know as she told anybody."

"I think she must have told Mead," Carey said drily. "From your question, I believe, Mr Silver, you may be thinking what I am."

"Sir?"

Carey looked from Jacob to Sarah. He appeared to be coming to a decision, and Jacob didn't want to guess wrongly what that might be. Finally the inspector cleared his throat.

"If Mead was pressuring or threatening Martyn, he must have had a weapon with which to do so," he said. "As I understand it, he is a buyer and seller of fleeces, doing business on a regular basis with Martyn, so he wouldn't jeopardize his own livelihood by making an empty threat, simply to save a girl's job. The only way he could do that is by having knowledge of something Martyn wouldn't want made public. Miss Simm has just told us of an event that fits that description."

"I assume," Jacob said thoughtfully, "the girl in question was not Mead's daughter or niece, since he was trying to help her, and Sarah says her family were indifferent, even hostile, to her problems. Or to be more precise, Mead was using her situation to put pressure on Martyn. So Martyn must have known not only of the girl's pregnancy but also have had a good idea of the child's paternity."

"I agree," Carey said. "Which leads me to believe that Martyn himself might have been responsible."

Bell, who had been so silent they had nearly forgotten his presence, suddenly spoke up.

"Could have been him," he said. "But more likely, I reckon, to be his son."

Jacob nodded. From the little contact he had had with the two men, Nathaniel seemed arrogant and conceited enough to impregnate a young girl and then deny all knowledge. And his father, despite his disapproval of Nathaniel's lifestyle, might have defended him to protect the family name.

But in that case, Jacob thought, it should have been Mead, not Martyn, lying dead under the fallen branch.

Carey turned to Bell, who looked rather nervous at having made his suggestion.

"Sergeant, two tasks for you. First, ask Dr Sheridan if he knows whether Sally Wright was pregnant. We might have a case of history repeating itself here. After that, go to the workhouse and see if the girl who had the child is still there, and if not, where she might have gone. Miss Simm, what is her name?"

"I only know her Christian name, sir."

"Which is?"

"Mary."

"All right. Off you go, Sergeant, and report to me when you've learned something."

"Yes, sir." Bell got to his feet and nodded to the other three before going out.

"I wish I hadn't had to tell you," Sarah said. "I don't reckon it's got anything to do with Sally Wright and whoever killed her."

"Not directly, perhaps," Carey said. "But at least we now have a better idea of why Mead was threatening Thomas Martyn, and if that leads either to his conviction or his release, it will have been worth breaking a confidence. Although I imagine the pregnancy and its aftermath were known to quite a few people."

"Not that many, sir. Somethin' like that, you wouldn't tell a soul unless you had to. I kind of found out by accident, hearing some girls talkin'. If she'd got her job back, nothin' might have been said. It was when she didn't come back that people got to know about it."

"Yes, I can see that. It's a shame Thomas Martyn didn't realize that; it may have saved his life. Now, Miss Simm, although you have been helpful in possibly clearing up one aspect of the Martyn case, I am still in the dark as to why anyone would want to kill either you or Sally Wright. Can you help me at all with that?"

Sarah shook her head.

"I don't know, honest, sir. I never did nothin' to make anyone hate me that bad. And I don't know nothin' to make anyone think I'm goin' to shop 'em, either."

"I am delighted to hear you aren't stooping to blackmail," Carey said. "But sometimes people know things they aren't aware of, if you understand me. Something you may have seen or heard, which meant nothing to you at the time, but would constitute a threat if interpreted correctly."

"I've been thinkin' and thinkin'," Sarah said, "but I've not seen or heard anything like that. I'm sure of it, sir."

Carey tried again but got more negative responses, and Jacob believed Sarah was as puzzled as the inspector, since she would have no reason not to divulge an enemy's name if she knew of one. And she was intelligent enough to know if she had witnessed anything remotely questionable which could have been turned to ammunition for blackmail.

Finally Carey made a gesture of resignation.

"I must get on with other inquiries," he said. "Thank you for your help, and if you should think of anything I should know, please tell me."

"Yes, sir, we will," Jacob said. He saw the inspector out and returned to the parlor, where to his astonishment, Sarah was wiping her eyes with the corner of her apron. Crying was simply not something she did, at least not in his presence.

"Sarah, don't cry," he said. "You'll be safe enough, I promise. And the inspector knows his job – he'll find out who killed Sally, and Thomas Martyn, for that matter."

Sarah sniffed and let the apron drop.

"I know, sir. Sorry, sir. I just wish I could *do* something. I feel bad enough tellin' him about Mary, but I hate this, feelin' like I'm waitin' for something bad to happen."

"It won't," Jacob said, hoping he was telling the truth. "Let's have some supper now and talk of more cheerful subjects."

As he had hoped, the idea of having something definite to do cheered Sarah. He knew she felt guilty about revealing Mary's plight, but Carey was right – if the story was accurate, it explained some of the inconsistencies in Mead's actions. He might have been acting from selfish motives, for example, demanding money to keep quiet about the paternity, or he might have genuinely had the girl's best interests at heart. Either way, it possibly explained why he had been so reluctant to provide himself with an alibi. He would have kept his crucial knowledge to himself until faced with an actual charge of murder, at which point he would have revealed Nathaniel's role.

They ate their supper of fish, potatoes and cabbage, carefully ignoring the subjects of murder and the plight of unmarried mothers, and then Sarah washed the crockery and pans. She was drying them when the sound came from the street of horses' hooves and carriage wheels, slowing and then stopping outside the house. Since residents at this end of Corn Street generally didn't use any transport other than their own feet, they both were suddenly alert.

Sarah froze in place, the linen towel in her hands. Jacob said quietly, "Give me the towel and go upstairs. Don't say anything and don't come down unless I call you."

She hurried up the stairs. Jacob folded the towel neatly and placed it on the rack, his ears cocked to hear if the carriage was going to continue. Instead, he heard footsteps and then a single sharp rap on the door. He went to answer it, opening it cautiously.

A woman he had never seen before stood on the step, a liveried driver waiting at the gate behind her. She was around thirty years old, he estimated, with fair hair and blue eyes, and dressed entirely in black from her hat to her boots.

"Jacob Silver?" she asked, in a tone that made Jacob think she wouldn't have taken 'no' for an answer.

"Yes, ma'am. May I be of service?"

"I am Mrs Charlotte Worth. Thomas Martyn's daughter. I wish to see your housemaid, Sarah Simm."

"I'm afraid she is not able to see you at the moment," Jacob said. "May I give her a message?"

After a pause so slight it was hardly noticeable, she said, "Yes, you may. Tell her I wish her to work in my household in Oxford. Beaumont Street. I shall be returning home tomorrow and shall expect her to present herself there on Wednesday."

SEVENTEEN

At first Jacob wasn't sure he had heard her correctly, but the glint in her eyes told him he had. He had absolutely no intention of letting Sarah work for this woman, even if she'd been willing to, so he said politely, "I will give her your message, Mrs Worth. Will there be anything else?"

Her gaze swept down the narrow hallway and took in what she could see of the small kitchen through the open door. Her lip curled slightly and she said, "No, there isn't. I am sure she will find it to her advantage to take up the post."

There didn't seem to be any point in further discussion, so Jacob inclined his head as Charlotte Worth turned and walked back to her carriage, and was handed into it by the silent driver. He waited until it had pulled away down the street before going to the foot of the stairs.

"Sarah?"

"Yes, sir?"

"You may come down now."

Sarah descended the stairs and stood looking at him, wide-eyed.

"Did you hear what Mrs Worth said?" he asked her.

"Yes, sir. Do I have to go work for her?"

"Of course not. She can't order you about like that, and I wouldn't agree to it anyway."

Sarah let out a sigh of relief. "Ta, Mr Silver. I don't want to leave here."

"I am pleased to hear that, since I suspect Mrs Worth's motives in offering you a post are not entirely generous."

"So what does she want with me? I'm not the kind of maid someone like her would want in their house, am I? She'd want someone with more class, someone more … "

"Obedient?" Jacob suggested with a smile. "No, you're quite correct. And tomorrow I will tell Inspector Carey of her request."

"Sounded more like an order to me," Sarah said.

"Yes, it did. She is very arrogant, and her offer is entirely without foundation."

"Sir?"

"You're not looking for a new post, so why should she offer you one? For that matter, I doubt she actually needs a new housemaid."

Sarah pondered this and said, "If she was a kinder person, I might think it was to make up for the way her pa treated my ma. But I don't think she's that sort, and besides, it's way too late for that."

"Yes. So there's some other reason, and it may have something to do with her father's death. I will let the inspector know what she said."

"There's something else comes to mind," Sarah said. "Being as it's only a few days since her pa died, she and her ma both would be stoppin' at home and not goin' out anywhere 'cept to church, not for months, maybe. So she waited 'til it was dark to come here, so no one but the carriage driver knew she'd been."

She was correct, of course. Jacob was well aware of the prolonged mourning period required by polite society for women, even in a small market town. Martyn's widow would not be going out in public for up to a year, and would wear mourning clothes even longer. She might attend church services and receive an occasional caller, but that was all.

As his daughter, Charlotte Worth would not be expected to mourn publicly for quite so long, but going out to recruit a new housemaid two days after her father's funeral was clearly a breach of accepted behavior.

"You're right, Sarah," he said. "And creeping around here after dark makes her behavior look even more questionable. So I think Inspector Carey will be very interested to hear of her visit."

It wasn't until much later that a more ominous thought came into Jacob's mind. If Sally Wright's murder had been a case of mistaken identity, and the murderer knew he or she had made a dreadful mistake, then taking Sarah to Oxford might lead to a second attempt to harm her. Try as he might, he couldn't rid himself of the notion that having failed to kill her, they were now trying to take her alive.

Jacob awoke the following morning with only one thought on his mind – had Inspector Carey made enough progress to arrest someone for Sally Wright's murder? He was relieved to hear activity in the kitchen as he washed and dressed, having worried that somehow Sarah would have been kidnapped or attacked without his knowledge during the night.

When he arrived in the kitchen, however, there was no sign that anything was amiss. Sarah was brewing tea and gave him a bright smile.

"Morning, Mr Silver."

"Good morning, Sarah. Did you sleep well?"

"You mean, am I frettin' about that Mrs Worth? No, I'm not. You say as I can stop here, so I will. If she tries anything, I'll go to the inspector. He thinks I'm clever; he said so."

"You *are* clever," Jacob said, "but you're also impetuous and headstrong at times. That means you act first and think later. And we are dealing with someone who has killed two people, so don't be too cocky."

He smiled to take the sting out and Sarah put an egg into the saucepan to boil.

"I'll be careful, sir. I ain't stupid."

"Good. Mrs Tucker will be here shortly, and after I've had my breakfast, I will go to the police station and tell Inspector Carey about Mrs Worth's visit last night. As for you, Sarah, the same rules apply as yesterday. Don't answer the door to strangers and if you go to the market, keep your eyes open and stay where there are other people. If you receive a message asking you to leave the house to go somewhere, ignore it. And do not go anywhere near the Martyns' house. Is that understood?"

"Yes, sir."

"I have a watch to take to a customer as well, so I may be some time."

"Yes, sir."

He wasn't entirely sure he trusted her to obey, but he consoled himself that she was accustomed to looking after herself, and with luck she would still be alive and unharmed when he returned. Mrs Tucker arrived as he was finishing his breakfast, so he felt better about delivering the watch while the two of them tackled the housework.

He walked up Corn Street and turned into Church Green, casting a covert eye at the Martyns' house on the far side. There was a flurry of activity at the front gate, perhaps the result of Charlotte Worth preparing to return to Oxford, or Martyn's sister setting off for Birmingham. A trunk was being loaded onto the back of a carriage and a swirl of black skirts told him the carriage's female passenger was also embarking.

Jacob caught a glimpse of Nathaniel at the side of the carriage, speaking to the woman inside, but from this distance, and with a black hat covering most of her hair and a veil over her eyes, he couldn't be sure who it was.

With a conscious need for haste, Jacob turned toward the police station, and encountered Carey on the front steps, obviously on his way out.

"I need to speak to you, Inspector," he said without preamble, then added, "if you have a minute, that is. I believe it's important."

"We're moving Mead to Oxford Prison today, so I'm rather busy," Carey said. He took another look at Jacob's tense expression. "Very well, Mr Silver. What is it?"

"I think we would be well advised to speak inside the station," Jacob said, glancing across the green.

Carey frowned, but held the door open and Jacob followed him inside.

"Last night, Charlotte Worth, Thomas Martyn's daughter, came to my house after dark," he said. "She ordered Sarah to go to Oxford tomorrow to work for her. I thought it an extraordinary thing for her to do, for several reasons, and I thought you should know."

"Thank you. I agree it was an odd thing to do. And is Miss Simm planning to go?"

"Of course not. She doesn't want to go, and I would forbid it if she did."

"Good." Carey moved toward the door.

"Is that all?" Jacob asked in surprise.

"For the moment, yes."

"I ask because I believe Mrs Worth may be preparing to go to Oxford now." He gestured across the green, where the carriage was now being turned around in readiness to leave.

"Don't worry, Mr Silver," Carey said calmly. "I know where to find her, should it become necessary."

Jacob wasn't completely reassured, but he supposed it was a reasonably courteous way of telling him to mind his own business and let the police handle theirs. After all, Oxford had its own small police force and there couldn't be very many doctors named Worth living in Beaumont Street.

"Thank you for your time, Inspector," he said, mustering a smile. "Like you, I have matters I need to attend to."

He used the time it took him to walk to Cogges to mull over the events of the past few days and try to put his jumbled thoughts in order. He had the feeling there was some common thread running through them, but the precise way they were tied together eluded him. The most mysterious part, he had to admit, was why anyone would want to harm Sarah, who although she occasionally exasperated him, couldn't be seen to pose a threat to anyone.

By the time he crossed the Windrush and arrived in the hamlet, he had almost decided that Sheridan had been mistaken, and that Sally Wright had been the intended victim all along, and that her death was the result of a robbery or seduction gone terribly wrong. But in that case, why did Charlotte Worth want Sarah in her household? To harm her, or to keep her away from something or someone in Witney? Neither made sense.

Jacob found the house of his customer, a rather fluttery elderly woman who was delighted to hear that her watch had merely needed routine cleaning and oiling and that his bill would be moderate. She paid him on the spot, leaving him equally relieved that he wouldn't have to chase his payment, as so often happened.

Feeling more cheerful, he wished her good day and started back toward Witney, only to stop on the footpath as an idea struck him. He turned around, and a few minutes later, he was approaching the stone church that served the inhabitants of the hamlet.

He hesitated outside its door and held a short internal debate before deciding that since he wasn't entering the church for purposes of worship, there was no good reason why he shouldn't go inside. He pushed the heavy wooden door open slowly, hoping no one would be present and he could find the information he wanted without anyone asking what he was doing.

The interior was dim, cold, and smelled of candlewax and stone dust. Stifling a sneeze, Jacob stood at the rear of the church and looked around him. Several rows of wooden pews lined either side of the central aisle which led to the altar. Some flowers badly in need of replacing flanked it, and on one side, Jacob was pleased to see a small table holding a thick leather-bound book, in which he hoped the parish records would be recorded.

He moved quickly up the side aisle, casting another glance around to make sure he was alone and that no one would burst out of the small vestry demanding to know his business. He opened the book carefully and sent up a silent prayer of his own when he saw that it did indeed record the christenings, weddings and funerals that held been held in the church.

Because it was a small parish, there weren't many entries for each month, perhaps two or three christenings, a wedding or two, the occasional confirmation and a handful of funerals, especially during the winter months. Jacob turned the pages, recognizing local names, and in the previous December, he found the entries for the deaths and funerals of Anne Simm and John Simm, Sarah's mother and brother.

The two funerals had been held a week apart, and Jacob felt a pang of sympathy for Sarah, having to cope with this double blow on her own. John had been ten years old at the time of his death, Jacob noted, and Anne had been thirty-one. That made him pause, as he did the arithmetic, realizing that meant Anne had been only seventeen when Sarah was born. But that was not too unusual; many women were married and gave birth to their first child before they were twenty.

He continued to turn pages, with the sensation that he was moving backward through time. Three years ago, as Sarah had told him, James Edward Simm, aged thirty-six, had died and his funeral held. He moved back five years ago, then ten. At this point, he found the christening of John James Simm. He turned another few pages. Then he stopped, his finger resting on an entry from twelve years previously. This one recorded the marriage between Anne Elizabeth Porter, spinster, and James Edward Simm, bachelor.

The wedding had been twelve years ago, and Sarah was fourteen.

Jacob couldn't have said how long he stood there, staring at the entry, written in neat copperplate by – he supposed – either the vicar or a parish clerk. Sarah had no reason to lie about her age, so no matter how he calculated it, the evidence was clear that Sarah's parents had not been married at the time she was born.

He wondered if she was aware of the fact. She had never indicated that she knew she was illegitimate, or perhaps she didn't care. She carried her father's name, so if her parents had not married until after her birth – well after it, according to the record – she might not have thought it important.

With a feeling of unreality, he turned the pages back still further, until he was looking at the month in which Sarah had been born. Then he worked forward again through the next few months, looking for a christening of a child called Sarah. There wasn't one. Had she been denied a christening because of her illegitimate birth? Or was there some other reason?

Jacob closed the book, making sure to leave it exactly as he had found it. Then he walked back out of the church, pausing to drop a few pennies in the charity box just inside the door before he closed it. It had been worth the money to learn what he had just seen, even though he was not yet sure what it meant.

A small man wearing a clerical collar and a determined expression passed him on the path, and Jacob was thankful he hadn't been caught perusing the parish records. There was no real reason why he shouldn't have, but as a non-Christian, he was certain he would have been accused of some heretical crime. As it was, he merely nodded politely to the vicar and continued on his way.

Sarah had told him she didn't attend the Cogges church because it reminded her of her mother and brother's funerals, but he now suspected that wasn't the reason, or at least not the complete reason. She hadn't felt welcome, and now he knew the probable cause.

Lost in thought as he walked, he was nearly back to Church Green before he realized there was a very plausible, if unsavory, explanation for the mystery surrounding Sarah's birth.

Annie Porter had left the Martyns' household, ostensibly to get married. That, at least, was the story Sarah had been told. But what if she had been dismissed for the same reason many maids lost their positions – because she was expecting a child? That would explain why Thomas Martyn had refused to let her return even after her husband died, given his views on moral behavior. He probably thought she was a shameless hussy, who had become pregnant through her own wanton behavior.

The situation certainly had echoes of Mary the factory girl, and her situation. But given the strong possibility that Nathaniel Martyn was responsible for Mary's pregnancy, wasn't it possible that there had been others over the years? Fifteen years earlier, when Anne Porter had become pregnant while living in the Martyn household, she would have been sixteen, and Nathaniel perhaps a year or two older. Judging by Sarah's appearance, her mother had probably been an attractive girl, one to catch the eye of the younger son of the house, but not able to object if he'd taken advantage of her.

If Jacob's theory was correct, then Anne had been more fortunate than most girls in that position, in that she had later married a man who had accepted her child and not condemned her for something that likely was not her fault at all.

Since Evangeline Martyn would have been managing the household and its staff, Thomas Martyn might not have been aware of his son's actions over the years. If Evangeline suspected what her son had done, she wouldn't have let on, or even told her husband. She would have felt he had more important things to concern him, such as the running of the factory, and wouldn't have bothered him with something as minor as a pregnant maid. It had taken Jerome Mead, threatening to make Mary's pregnancy and the child's paternity public, to open his eyes.

It fitted together only too well, Jacob thought. The only real difficulty would be telling Sarah that Nathaniel Martyn, the obnoxious man who had accused them both of theft and wanted them arrested, might be her father.

EIGHTEEN

Because he knew it would be an awkward conversation, Jacob decided to delay speaking to Sarah. She would have to know, of course, but it would be better to be absolutely sure of his facts before he told her, or as sure as he could be. He couldn't believe she had any idea of her possible paternity – her frequent critical comments about Nathaniel were proof of that.

He found himself wandering down the High Street with no real idea of where he was going. He passed Sheridan's surgery and reminded himself to find out if the doctor had known whether or not Sally Wright had been pregnant when she died.

He passed the greengrocery, instinctively keeping an eye open for flying turnips or potatoes. The High Street became Bridge Street as it crossed the river, and he could see the footpath where Sally had died.

And finally, without conscious thought, he found himself staring at the three balls suspended above the door of Josiah Morton's pawnshop.

Morton was just visible inside, arranging his wares in a case to entice buyers. Jacob could see jewelry and clocks, possibly ones he had repaired himself, set on black cloth to display them to the best advantage. He pushed the door open.

"Well, well, what an honor," Morton said, straightening up. "What can I do for you, Silver? I assume you've come to ask a favor, since you're far too wealthy to need to pawn anything."

"I'm afraid my finances are not nearly as robust as you may think," Jacob said. "But you are quite right about the favor. I wanted to ask you a question."

"Yes?" Morton's rat-like face showed no particular emotion.

"On the day of Thomas Martyn's funeral, you told me his son Nathaniel had pawned various objects with you."

"Yes. He did."

"Has he redeemed any of them since his father's death?"

"No, no. Probably won't bother now." Morton's invisible whiskers quivered. "I hear the will was read yesterday, so he knows he'll be coming into a fine inheritance soon. He won't need the likes of me once he's got that, more's the pity."

"So the objects he pawned are still here?"

"Didn't I just say they were?"

"So you did. May I see them?"

Morton nodded without comment and went to one of his cases, sliding the door open. He removed several items and laid them on the counter where Jacob could inspect them. A pocket watch – far inferior to the one his father had left with Jacob – was one of them, along with a signet ring, a small silver vase, a round glass paperweight, a cigar cutter and two miniature portraits.

Jacob bent over and studied these last two items closely. They were obviously intended as a pair, portraying a young man and a young woman, who judging from their resemblance to each other, were brother and sister. The artist had been skillful, capturing the personalities as well as the features of his subjects, even though each picture was no more than four by six inches.

"I am surprised he would pawn these," he said. "They must be family portraits and would be missed."

"No idea," Morton said. "It's not my business to ask whether he had permission."

"Of course not. When did he leave them?"

Morton didn't answer, but instead went to a book under his counter and opened it, turning the pages until he found the entry.

"A fortnight ago," he said. "No, I tell a lie. Three weeks come tomorrow."

About the same time Jacob had returned the watch to Nathaniel's father, then.

"And he has not come back or sent word that he will redeem them?"

"No."

"Would you sell them to me?"

Morton shot him a shrewd look, as if to calculate Jacob's motives, but said only, "Why not?"

After a brief but amiable haggling session, Jacob left the shop, the portraits wrapped in brown paper and tucked into his coat pocket. It had taken a large portion of the money from his Cogges customer to pay for them, but he didn't regret his purchase, not when they might play a crucial role in unraveling a mystery.

He walked back up the High Street and turned into Corn Street, his thoughts in turmoil, and almost dreading the task he had to do. He arrived at his house to find Mrs Tucker just leaving, making her way across the small garden and down the lane behind the house.

Sarah was in the kitchen, and he paused in the doorway, watching her and wondering how to approach a distasteful subject. She turned and smiled at him.

"Get your business done, sir? Me and Mrs Tucker, we've aired out all the rooms and scrubbed the downstairs floors, so mind how you go. You don't want to slip and fall on them wet stones."

"I'll be careful," Jacob said, ignoring her question. He took the two portraits from his pocket and placed them on the table.

"What you got there, then, Mr Silver?"

"Something I bought from Morton, the pawnshop owner. Two small oil paintings, portraits."

Sarah's face plainly showed her opinion of spending good money on a pair of paintings, but she came around to look at them, and slowly her expression cleared. She pointed to the painting of the young woman and looked up at Jacob.

"That's that Mrs Worth, ain't it? I saw her from the top of the stairs. This'd be a few years back, mind, but she's not changed that much."

"No, she hasn't. A trifle more arrogant now, I think, but nothing more."

"Arr, you can see even when she were a girl, she'd like to have her own way."

"I daresay she did. She still does, as you know."

Sarah turned her attention to the other portrait. "So who's this? He looks like her, but it's not Mr Nathaniel. This lad's too friendly to be him."

Jacob smiled. Sarah was right – the young man in the painting, perhaps seventeen or eighteen years old at the time, had a far more gracious expression than Nathaniel had ever displayed in Jacob's presence. Of course, he had no reason to be polite to a Jewish tradesman, but good manners, if nothing else, would have required it of one claiming to be a gentleman. This young man, however, looked as though he would display courtesy naturally, not because it was expected.

"I think it must be Thomas Martyn's older son, Frederick," he said. "He told me Frederick died of typhoid when he was nineteen, so perhaps not long after this portrait was painted."

"That's a pity," Sarah said. "Would have been better the other way around, wouldn't it? I don't think Mr Nathaniel would be missed much, not from what Gracie says."

"No, Frederick – if that's who this is – looks a much more pleasant person than his younger brother. Who, we must remember, is now the head of the family."

Sarah wrinkled her nose, a silent but eloquent comment on Nathaniel's personality.

"Wonder why there's no painting of him, when there's one of his brother and sister."

"Perhaps there is, and he keeps it elsewhere. Or perhaps he wouldn't sit still long enough to be painted."

She gave a little chuckle and said, "This Mr Frederick, he's handsome, ain't he? Expect he had some young ladies havin' high hopes of him once he was old enough to be wed."

Jacob stared at her. He looked down at Frederick's portrait again, noting the blue eyes, the light brown hair and the slight smile that had seemed familiar as soon as he had seen it, although he hadn't been sure why. Now he knew.

He wondered if Sarah herself noticed the resemblance, given that she had little time to study her own reflection in a looking glass. But this made sense, in a way that his previous idea had not, and explained so many things, such as the way Sarah's accent veered from one class to another. She must have unconsciously copied it from her mother, who in turn had picked up certain vocabulary and pronunciations from her employer's son.

If nothing else, he was thankful to see Nathaniel receding into the background as a potential parent. And there was a simple way of testing his theory.

"Sarah," he said, "when you were pretending to be a young lad, you called yourself Fred. Why did you choose that name?"

She gasped as she looked at the painting again, and he could tell that she immediately grasped the significance of the question.

Her eyes, so like the ones in the portrait, widened and she said slowly, "Ma used to tell me that if I'd been a boy, she'd have named me Fred. And she always had a kind of sad face when she said it. Oh my goodness, Mr Silver, you don't suppose it could be, do you, that Mr Frederick was my real pa? And that would mean Mr Martyn – he'd have been my grandfather."

"I don't know," Jacob said, thankful that he hadn't had to spell out his theory in detail. "And I don't know how you could find out, not after this long. Did you never think that James Simm might not have been your true father?"

She shook her head. "He was always just my pa. A good man, he was. Ask anyone, and they'd tell you Jamie Simm was honest, worked hard and didn't do anything he ought not to have done. We was always poor, but he didn't get drunk, didn't beat Ma and always treated me and Johnny good."

"I think he was a very good man, and your mother must have been grateful to him," Jacob said. "If he hadn't married her, she might have suffered a far worse fate. Because if Frederick Martyn *was* your father, I'm afraid he wouldn't have been allowed to even think about marrying a housemaid, no matter what passed between them. He might have been fond of Anne – even been in love with her – but the best he could have done would be to arrange some sort of financial support for her and their child. But then he died, so even that wasn't possible."

"I know," Sarah said soberly. "And Mr Martyn, with his high and mighty morals, he wouldn't have cared if she'd starved, or me, neither. Mr Silver, how'd you happen to come by this?"

She gestured toward the portraits, but he knew she meant the entire body of knowledge and speculation. He decided she deserved honesty – after all, it was her entire identity, her past and possibly her future they were discussing.

"I was in Cogges to see a customer and whilst I was there, I thought I'd visit the church," he said.

"But you're not a Christian. Why'd you go to the church?"

"I went because I wanted to look at the parish records."

"Oh. Why?"

"Curiosity, I suppose. And I found far more than I expected."

"About me?"

"Not exactly. I found that your parents hadn't been married until two years after you were born. Then I found your birth and christening hadn't been recorded. All right, you may have been christened elsewhere, but all the other family events had been in Cogges, so that was odd. I started to think about how young your mother had been when you were born and wondered if possibly Nathaniel had seduced her and caused her to lose her position in the household."

"Like Mary in the factory," Sarah said. "Expect he might have tried it, if he could. Gracie says you have to watch yourself when he's about, even now."

It took Jacob a moment to realize Sarah was hinting that Nathaniel – only a little older than himself – was too decrepit to want to pursue women any longer. He smiled inwardly and hurried on.

"Yes, as Mary may have found out to her cost. I had some idea of trying to speak to someone who would have been familiar with the Martyn household fifteen years ago, to see if it was a possibility, but then I saw those portraits in Morton's pawnshop. I knew Nathaniel had pawned them, but assumed it was for ready money. Now I think perhaps he had another reason."

Sarah nodded. "He didn't want them in the house, 'cause someone might have noticed that girl who comes round to talk to Gracie sometimes – and that cheeky lad who calls himself Fred – they both look a lot like his dead brother."

"So what do we do now?" Sarah asked. She had turned to the usual solution for dealing with crises by boiling the kettle and setting the tea to brew, and now they were seated at the pine table with two steaming cups. The Martyn family portraits lay on the table in front of them.

"I honestly don't know," Jacob said. "I will put the paintings in a safe place, but I think for the time being it would be better not to mention this to anyone. Especially not to anyone connected with the Martyn household."

"Yes, but Mrs Worth, she's expectin' me to start workin' for her tomorrow. What do you think she'll do when I don't?"

Jacob didn't know the answer to that question, either.

"'Cause if what you think is true, then she'd be my aunt, wouldn't she? Funny sort of thing, having your niece be your maid, even if she were born on the wrong side of the blanket."

"But a good way of keeping a close watch on you," he said. "Inspector Carey and Sergeant Bell are in Oxford today, taking Jerome Mead to the prison there. It's possible they may call on Mrs Worth whilst they are there, to ask her why she commanded you to work for her. If she learns the police know of her actions, she may not pursue it any further."

He glanced at the determined expression of the girl in the portrait, and hoped he was correct.

"But why are they takin' Mead to prison? They know as he didn't kill that Sally, and maybe not Mr Martyn, either."

"He didn't tell me, and I'm in no position to insist on an explanation. Either they have found some more evidence linking him to Martyn's death, or they're moving him for his own safety. The police station here isn't very secure, and as I know all too well, the townspeople can be easily whipped up into a violent mob."

"Arr, and that were only vegetables," Sarah said. "Could have been worse."

"And when the inspector returns," Jacob said, ignoring her comment, "I will speak to him again."

Sarah shifted uneasily in her chair. "Will you tell him what you think, sir? About Mr Frederick maybe being my pa?"

"I think I may have to tell him. He'll have much more chance of finding some proof, one way or another, if he knows. I'm sorry, Sarah."

He could see her attempting a nonchalant attitude, a commendable one given that her entire world had just been turned upside down.

"Doesn't matter, I guess. Jamie Simm's the only pa I ever knew or ever will know. And better that Mr Frederick's the one, rather than Mr Nathaniel, if it comes to that."

"Yes, indeed," Jacob said. "Mrs Rexford spoke highly of him, that day she fed me the scones and gossip. His father clearly preferred him as well."

Sarah drank her tea.

"You know, what I can't understand," she said, setting the cup down, "is why this is all happenin' all of a sudden. If – and I know it's only *if* – Mr Frederick and my ma were … you know … together, somebody must have known about it years ago. But nobody said anythin', did they?"

"I expect it was because Frederick died of typhoid about then," Jacob said. "That solved a delicate problem, in a way, because the Martyns could dismiss your mother on the basis of her pregnancy and Frederick wouldn't be there to protest on her behalf."

"So what I mean," Sarah persisted, "is that nobody said anythin' about it, even when Mr Martyn was stabbed. We still don't know why he was stabbed, do we? Then all of a sudden, this Sally Wright gets killed, maybe 'cause someone thought she was me, and Mrs Worth is orderin' me to work for her. Why? Is it 'cause she wants me to be in Oxford, or 'cause there's some reason she don't want me to be in Witney?"

"That's a good question," Jacob said, realizing he hadn't viewed it that way. He had been so sure Charlotte Worth intended to harm Sarah that he hadn't considered she might be simply trying to get her away from … what? Or who?

"Something happened to change things," he said, half to himself. "The murder of Sally Wright, Mrs Worth's clandestine visit here – both of those could be seen as attempts to remove you from Witney, one temporarily and one permanently. And they both happened after Thomas Martyn's funeral. So what could have …"

He suddenly sat bolt upright as an idea struck him. He remembered Mrs Rexford commenting that Thomas Martyn had been to see her husband a few days before his death, as if, she had said, he had a premonition of his death. He recalled Morton saying that Nathaniel would have learned of his inheritance when the will was read.

And finally he remembered Martyn's harried appearance when he had left that fine, valuable watch with Jacob for safekeeping. Martyn saying he hoped he was wrong about something – possibly the fact he feared his life was in danger? Well, he had certainly been correct about that.

And those other words, which had made no sense at the time. *Instructions will be sent.*

Legal instructions, perhaps, contained in a will which had only just been read to the family?

"I have a feeling," he said, "that although he may not have known exactly who or where you were, he knew Frederick had a child, and he may have made some sort of provision for you in his will. So, Sarah, you may possibly inherit something from Thomas Martyn's estate."

NINETEEN

"I think he had just found out about your existence," Jacob continued. "He may not have known your name, where you lived or anything else about you. But he learned – somehow – that his favorite son had fathered a child, and if nothing else, I wager he wanted you to have that watch. So he gave it to me for safekeeping, not realizing who you were and that you were already in this household. He may have instructed me to deliver it to you later, perhaps when you reach your majority."

"My what, sir?"

"When you are twenty-one years old and have some legal standing."

Sarah stared, and then burst into laughter. "You mean I could have pinched my own watch? Before I brought it back to you?"

"Possibly." There was an exquisite irony there, and Jacob smiled in appreciation.

"No wonder Mr Nathaniel was so keen to get it back. Fancy it goin' to someone like me. His pa must have told him what he was doin' with it."

"Well, it's only a theory. But it would explain several things, including his visit here. The way to make certain, of course, is to consult Mr Rexford and find out the terms of the will. I don't think you will be wealthy, but there may be some sort of provision made for you. A small annual income from the factory's profits, perhaps."

Sarah's eyes grew wide. "If there is, Mr Silver, don't think I'll be goin' off and givin' myself airs. No, I'll stop right here and work for you. If you don't mind, that is."

Jacob was touched by her loyalty. "Of course I don't mind, Sarah. This is your home for as long as you want to live here. But let's wait and see what Mr Rexford can tell us. I'll consult him tomorrow morning."

"So Mr Nathaniel would already know what's in that will," Sarah said. "And he's tryin' to keep me from finding out. Maybe even tryin' real hard to keep me from gettin' anything ever, by gettin' rid of me."

"Yes, but again, it's only a theory. But if it is true that you've been left anything substantial, I imagined Nathaniel would move heaven and earth to keep you from getting it. Frederick was the favored elder son, after all, so I doubt they were very close as boys. Killing Frederick's daughter wouldn't bother his conscience much, I fancy."

He wondered if he should have phrased his fears more tactfully. He had clashed with his own older brother on occasion, but the thought of murdering him – or his children – to enhance an inheritance would never have crossed his mind. Of course, there was far more at stake in the Martyn family, and Nathaniel undoubtedly had fewer scruples than Jacob.

"You reckon it was him killed Sally Wright, thinking she was me? He doesn't know me, not really."

Jacob had been thinking about that. "Did he see you at the funeral? Now that we know what Frederick looked like, we also know there's a strong resemblance between the two of you."

"Arr, but not up real close, and there was a lot of people there." Sarah considered. "No, I reckon it was one of them times when I was chattin' to Gracie and he happened to get a good look at me. He'd know me if he saw me again. But at night, walkin' along behind me and stayin' well back so's I'd not take any notice of him, I'd look much like Sally Wright. Or she'd look like me, poor soul."

"And Mrs Worth? Did she have a chance to see you clearly at the funeral?"

"Oh, my." Sarah set her cup down and looked straight at Jacob. "Never thought of that. You think a lady like her would dirty her hands stabbin' somebody? Think of the blood gettin' on that lovely black dress of hers."

"That would depend how much was at stake, I think. As you observed, she's a very determined woman. And a woman would have easier access to a kitchen where sharp knives were kept."

"Oh, arr." Sarah gave a little shiver. "Don't think I shall sleep much tonight, Mr Silver, what with all this happening. Me findin' out I may have a new pa, and maybe gettin' some money and a nice watch, and maybe someone tryin' to kill me as well, all in the same day. Never had that happen before."

She gave a mock grimace, but Jacob knew that under the bravado, she was genuinely worried, and he couldn't blame her a bit.

"I will lock and bolt the doors, I'll be here and you'll be quite safe," he said, trying for a confidence he didn't really feel. "In the morning, we'll go to Mr Rexford and try to make sense of it all. We may be completely mistaken, you know, about all of it."

"Hope you *are* mistaken, sir, in a way. I don't mind at all just bein' me, like I've always been."

The rest of the afternoon passed without further excitement, unless one counted the fact that Sarah was so preoccupied with her possible new future that she put sugar into the stew she was preparing for their supper in place of salt, and burnt the bread she was toasting. Jacob found her trying to strain out the broth to water it down and scrape the charred bits off the toast. He silently took the knife from her hand.

"Sarah, please don't worry. I'll look after you and we'll speak to Inspector Carey and Mr Rexford tomorrow."

"I ain't worried, sir." She glanced up at him. "Maybe a bit worried. Not about the money, mind. Won't miss what I've never had."

Jacob scraped the last of the charred toast and reached for the butter. He buttered two rounds of toast and placed them on the plates, then scooped two portions of thickened – and possibly sweetened – stew from the pan into bowls.

"Don't worry about the stew, Sarah; I'm sure it will be fine. Come and eat now, and you'll feel better."

As darkness fell, Jacob found himself growing ever more tense. It was one thing to calm Sarah's fears, but another to convince himself. He almost wished he had not gone to the church, not discovered the secret interwoven history of the Simm and Martyn families. He reminded himself that nothing was proven yet; that it was only an idea, a theory. And yet, from the moment Sarah's face had looked out at him from Frederick's portrait, he had known he was right.

The question, of course, was just how much Nathaniel and his sister knew, and what they planned to do about it. John Rexford had read the will that morning, and its contents might well provoke them to action. He doubted Thomas Martyn had left much to his newly discovered granddaughter, but would it be enough to commit murder for? Or was the disgrace of their brother's conduct – loving a girl he knew he could never marry – enough to tip them into violence?

He lit the lamps and sat at the table, brooding in silence, while Sarah watched him soberly. Whatever she thought of the situation, she seemed content to let him deal with it, a fact that made him even more tense. It was bad enough trying to survive the occasional abuse of his fellow citizens without having to protect a girl who might be the target of a killer.

Finally he said, "Go to bed, Sarah. I'll lock up."

She nodded, took a candle and said, "Good night, Mr Silver."

"Good night, Sarah." He managed a smile. "Sleep well."

"Doubt it," she said, with an attempt at cheerfulness. "But I'll try."

He watched her go upstairs, listening to the sound of her footsteps overhead as she got ready for bed. When they had subsided into silence, he went into his workshop and took Martyn's watch from the locked drawer. He brushed off the coal dust, put it into a small cloth bag, and tucked it into his jacket pocket.

Back in the kitchen, he took the two small portraits and placed them face to face, wrapping a linen napkin around them. They just fit in his other jacket pocket that way, and although it made walking a bit awkward, he felt it was better to keep them where he could get to them easily.

Then he checked yet again that the doors were locked and bolted, turned down the lamps and went upstairs. After a moment's thought, he pulled back the blanket and sheet and got into bed fully dressed except for his boots and jacket.

Tomorrow, he felt, could not come soon enough.

Jacob knew sleep would not come easily, but eventually he drifted into an uneasy slumber. At one point he woke to hear rain pattering on the roof, and chided himself for being so jumpy that the familiar sound seemed ominous.

He turned over and went back to sleep.

The next time he woke, it was because someone was shaking his shoulder. He opened his eyes and saw moonlight streaming through the window, and Sarah, dressed in the boy's trousers, jacket and cap, leaning over his bed.

"Mr Silver," she whispered, "someone's trying to get in the door. Listen."

Jacob sat up and listened. She was right; he could hear a scraping noise coming from the front of the house, directly below his bedroom window.

"Reckon we should go down?"

Jacob put his finger to his lips, and got out of bed as quietly as possible, moving to the window and looking down. He could see a shadowy figure at his door, but it was too dark to identify it, or even to tell if it was a man or a woman. He turned back to Sarah and spoke as softly as he could.

"I'll go down and have a look. Watch from the top of the stairs, and if I beckon, then come down and we'll go out the back door."

"Go where, sir?" she asked.

It was a reasonable question and Jacob hesitated before answering.

"Away from the house – I don't know where. They are probably after the watch, or maybe they intend to do some damage to my workshop or the house itself."

"More likely they want to do some damage to you and me, 'specially me."

That was all too possible. Jacob said, "I'll go down now, so watch for me to give you a signal."

Holding his boots in one hand and with his jacket over his arm, Jacob crept down the wooden stairs in his stocking feet, praying that no creak would give him away. He reached the bottom of the staircase, where he could hear someone trying to force the lock on the front door.

He knew that unless they had brought an ax with them, it would take an intruder some time to get past both the lock and the sliding bolt on the inside, and he was glad he had installed them after some incidents involving drunken revelers.

Once on the stone floor, he slid his feet into his boots and pulled his jacket on, buttoning it and feeling the weight of the watch and the portraits in the pockets. Then he looked up the staircase, where Sarah was standing, and beckoned to her. Like him, she carried her boots in her hand and came silently down the stairs to join him.

Together they moved quietly through the dark kitchen and then the scullery. Jacob eased the door open and looked out. The person at the front seemed to be the only intruder, so he stepped into the garden, with Sarah close behind him. They walked quickly across the grass and Jacob opened the gate on the far side, which led to the alley running behind the terraced houses.

Too late, he remembered that he had meant to oil the hinges on the wrought iron gate, which tended to creak when opened or shut. The gate gave a groan, and as Jacob and Sarah slipped through it and into the narrow alley, they heard footsteps hurrying around the side of the house.

It was one of the few times Jacob had regretted living on the end of the terrace – a house in the middle of the row would have bought him a little more time. As it was, he began running, with Sarah at his heels, thinking that at least this answered one question. The intruder wasn't after anything in the house; he or she wanted its occupants.

They ran the length of the alley, and as they reached the mouth, Sarah grabbed Jacob's arm and hissed, "Follow me."

He would have asked the obvious question, but common sense told him Sarah knew more than he did about Witney's back streets and lanes, and had more experience evading pursuers. So he allowed her to lead the way as they dodged through inn yards, hurried down cobbled alleys and at one point, scrambled over a five foot high dry stone wall, Jacob making a hasty step with his linked hands so she could reach the top.

The moonlight allowed them to see where they were going without much difficulty, but unfortunately it also allowed them to be seen as they fled, even though Sarah led them into deep shadows whenever possible. Jacob could hear that they were being followed the entire way, the pursuing footsteps sometimes fading, only to catch up again. He thought he could hear muffled curses at the wall, then boots hitting the stone as the person climbed over the same way he had, using the niches between the stones for purchase. Once he even thought he heard more than one set of footsteps behind them, but dismissed that as a product of his over-active imagination.

He had completely lost track of where they were, and began to think they had doubled back on themselves when they crossed a short expanse of grass and Sarah plucked at his sleeve.

"Down here. Slide."

He peered into the darkness, but Sarah was gone, her head disappearing from sight as she flew feet first down a slope. Jacob took a deep breath and followed her lead, half sitting and half lying on slippery wet grass as he slid.

It seemed as if he were sliding down a mountainside, but it was probably no more than ten or twelve feet before his progress was halted by a row of bushes. A small hand reached out and pulled him under one of them and he realized Sarah must have already known about this hiding place; she had undoubtedly hidden here before. The bush formed a natural barrier, the branches reaching nearly to the ground, where the two of them crouched without speaking.

He heard water rushing past and decided they must be near the river, and the slope had led down to the bank at the water's edge. He reached up and parted the branches enough to confirm this, and to his surprise, saw the bulk of the blanket factory rising nearby and the arch of the old stone bridge. So that was where they had ended up – just off the footpath where Sally Wright had died. He shivered, not from cold, and patted both his pockets to make sure his cargo had survived the chase.

It was intact, and he breathed easily for the first time in half an hour. Beside him, Sarah was listening, her face screwed up in concentration.

"I think we lost him," she murmured. "Can't hear anything."

"Good."

"So we'll wait here a while."

Jacob was amused at how she had taken charge of their flight, but he couldn't argue. She had been nimble enough to lose their follower, and crouching uncomfortably under a bush on wet grass was a small price to pay. What would happen next, he couldn't begin to imagine. It was unlikely anyone would find them under the bushes, but it also meant they couldn't summon help from anywhere. It would be embarrassing to be discovered by early morning workers on their way to the factory, assuming they were still hiding there at sunrise.

He had just decided to ease his aching legs by kneeling when he heard a brushing noise in the bushes beside them. Before he could determine whether it was an animal or something less welcome, a hand clamped itself firmly over his mouth and a second one grasped his wrist.

He looked sideways and saw Sarah struggling in someone else's grip.

"I'll turn you loose but don't make any loud noises," murmured a voice that Jacob thought he recognized. He nodded and the hand was removed.

He turned his head and in the moonlight filtering through the leaves, saw Inspector Carey crouched beside him.

"Who's the lad?" the inspector asked quietly, indicating Sarah, still being held by Sergeant Bell.

"I'm not a lad. It's me, Sarah."

Bell released her as if his hands had been scalded. Sarah glared at him and straightened her jacket and the cap which, despite all their activity, had remained on her head.

"Why is she dressed like that?" Bell muttered.

"We can discuss that later," Carey said irritably. "No doubt there's a reason."

"Of course," Jacob said, keeping his voice as low as possible. "But I thought you were in Oxford, sir, taking Mead to prison."

"Precisely what you and everyone else were supposed to think. Baiting a trap, you might say. You have your tools of the trade, and we have ours."

"I see. But why are you here? Were you following us?"

"No."

"Then why …"

"We were following the man who was following you," Carey said, "and I must say it would have made our lives easier if you had let him break into your house rather than leading everyone on a merry chase all over Witney. But with luck, he was concentrating on you too much to notice us. Now, Silver, listen to me. I need you to draw him out if you can, and we'll do the rest. But keep quiet, because he must not be far away."

Jacob was only too happy to obey. Carey and Bell moved backward into the shadows, leaving Jacob and Sarah under the bush. *Like tethered goats,* Jacob thought. *They'll wait until we're attacked and then move in. I only hope they move quickly enough.*

He felt Sarah's hand touch his, reminding him that despite her outward self-confidence, she was still very young and vulnerable. He closed his hand around hers. They waited. It seemed to be hours but eventually he heard rustling and someone crashing down the slope behind them far more noisily than he, Sarah or the police had done.

The crashing stopped and they could hear someone panting from unaccustomed exertion.

"I know you're under there, Silver," a voice said. "You're done for. You're a thief and I can prove it. No one will believe you. Come out."

He wasn't sure what Carey wanted him to do, but he let go of Sarah's hand and edged out to where he could just be seen, still in a half crouch as if trying to hide.

"That's right. Come out. I won't harm you; I just want what's mine."

Jacob stood up and parted the bushes. He took one step forward, just in time to see Nathaniel Martyn raise his arm. In his hand was a knife, the blade glittering in the moonlight.

TWENTY

Jacob thought he heard Sarah gasp, but if so, it was covered by the sound of the river. He held his hands out to demonstrate that he was not armed and Nathaniel laughed, a harsh, grating noise.

"Come to offer yourself as a sacrifice, have you? It won't work, Silver. I don't want to kill you, although I admit it wouldn't bother me to do it. No, I want the watch and I want the girl."

"What girl?" Jacob asked, pleased to hear that his voice remained steady.

"The one who works as your housemaid, or whatever else she does for you. That Sarah."

He let the slur go by. "Why do you want her? She's done nothing to harm you."

"No, not a thing," Nathaniel sneered. "She's done nothing but exist. Nothing but take what's mine by right. Nothing but turn my own father against me."

Jacob felt like replying that Nathaniel had done most of the damage himself, but he glanced at the knife and decided against it.

"She's done nothing to harm you," he repeated.

"I thought I'd got rid of her," Nathaniel said in an almost conversational tone. "Turned out it was some other little dolly mop called Sally who just looked like her."

He spoke as if Sally Wright had been nothing more than an annoying insect he had swatted, and Jacob was appalled.

"She was a human being. And another girl who'd not done you any harm."

"Oh, stop preaching at me," Nathaniel snapped. "You sound like my late, unlamented father, always telling me to mend my ways. Women are there to be taken, Silver. You're a man; you should understand that. But I wager you won't admit it, any more than my father did."

Jacob took a chance, hoping Carey could hear and was noting everything Nathaniel said.

"Did your father challenge you about the girl called Mary?" he asked.

"Mary? Who's Mary?"

"The one who lost her job at the factory after you made her pregnant. Surely you remember her?"

He was pleased to see this shook Nathaniel's confidence a bit. He scowled at Jacob and said, "Oh, yes, that one. Did that pest Mead tell you about her? Yes, he did tell my father, damn him. Just before he killed him."

"It's general knowledge in the town, what happened to Mary," Jacob said, hoping Carey would excuse the exaggeration. "And he may be a pest, but I don't think Jerome Mead killed your father, even though he has been arrested for the crime. And you know very well why I say that."

There was silence except for the sound of the river. Jacob and Nathaniel faced each other and Nathaniel pointed the knife at him, moving it from side to side menacingly.

"You not only talk too much, Silver, but you know too much. You'd never prove a thing, but I've changed my mind about letting you walk away. I know you weren't alone when you came here, so the girl must be somewhere about. And there's no point shouting for help. No one will hear you and that ignorant police inspector and his lapdog sergeant are in Oxford. Where is she?"

Jacob didn't answer.

"Where is she? Tell me. Or does she want to watch me kill you?"

Nathaniel's voice rose almost to the point of hysteria, and whatever self-control he possessed was rapidly disappearing. He raised the knife again and moved forward, while Jacob tried to calculate how best to dodge his downward strike. The bushes rustled behind him and he assumed it was Carey and Bell, preparing to pounce on their quarry now that he had done as they asked.

But to his astonishment, the branches parted and Sarah stepped forward, the moonlight making a faint halo around her. She said nothing, just gazed at Nathaniel, who took one look at her and then froze as if transfixed. Jacob fingered the portrait in his pocket, thinking how closely the young man in the painting resembled the slender figure in boys' clothing who stood beside him.

Nathaniel obviously had the same thought as he stared at her, his furious snarl melting into bewilderment and then into fear.

"Frederick?" he whispered. "Is that really you?"

Sarah nodded.

"Oh, my God."

Nathaniel wavered visibly. His arm dropped and Jacob lunged forward, grabbing his wrist and twisting it with all his strength until the knife dropped on the wet grass at his feet. Behind him, he heard Carey and Bell bursting from their hiding place, and was relieved to move aside to let them restrain Nathaniel, who was now making a high-pitched, inhuman whining noise. He finally tore his terrified gaze from Sarah's face as they manacled his hands behind his back and Bell stowed the knife safely in his belt.

The police officers steered Nathaniel away and Jacob turned to Sarah, still standing motionless in the moonlight. He put his arm around her shoulders, heedless of whether it was proper or appropriate.

"That was an extremely brave thing to do, Sarah," he said softly. "Your father – both of your fathers – would have been proud of you."

"Ta," she said, her voice quivering. "I dunno what made me think of it, pretendin' to be Frederick. It just come to me and I thought maybe he'd think I was a ghost or something, come back to haunt him for all the dreadful things he'd done, and it'd scare him enough for you to get away or give the inspector a chance to grab him."

She smiled shakily. "Good thing he didn't stop to think Frederick was a lot taller and wouldn't have worn ratty old clothes like these."

"I think he was beyond rational thought, to be honest."

Sarah gestured toward Nathaniel, who was now being marched away down the footpath. "What'll happen to him, Mr Silver?"

"He will be arrested and charged with murder. Two murders, that is, then taken to prison to await trial."

He felt no need to say that after they had all heard his public confession of Sally Wright's murder, Nathaniel could be looking forward to a rapid trip to the gallows or – an only slightly less terrifying prospect – commitment to an insane asylum. His family would hire the best legal representation possible, but it would be unlikely to save him.

"Two murders? You reckon he killed his own pa, then, as well as Sally Wright?"

"I think so, yes. He more or less told me so. Probably with the same knife he threatened me with, the one Sergeant Bell took away."

"Was it because of me?"

Jacob debated. He didn't want her to feel guilty, but she deserved to know the truth and was intelligent enough to sense if he was lying to her.

"I don't think it was completely because of you, Sarah. Nathaniel was a great disappointment to his father, and Thomas Martyn frequently let him know that. Perhaps the night of the storm, he finally said or did something which tipped Nathaniel over the edge. It may have had to do with Frederick, or Mary's situation or simply Nathaniel's bad behavior, especially toward women. Perhaps Martyn even told his son that he had changed his will to make a provision for you.

"I don't know exactly what was said, of course, but I would guess that they went outside so that their argument wouldn't be overheard in the household and argued or fought outside the front door of the family home. Nathaniel had a knife and stabbed him, panicked, and then realized he could use that fallen branch to cover him and with luck, the bloodstains would be attributed to the branch hitting and killing him."

"But Dr Sheridan was too clever to believe that."

"Yes, he was. You're shivering, Sarah."

"I know. Don't know why, though. It ain't that cold."

Jacob knew it was reaction setting in; now that the danger had passed, the body was catching up with the mind that had dealt with the immediate crisis.

In an effort to lighten her mood he asked, "What made you decide to be Fred tonight? I admit it was extremely useful, but how did you know he'd be needed?"

She gave him a sideways glance. "I didn't, but I don't think you've ever tried running anywhere in a dress, have you, sir? Real easy to trip and fall, and as for climbin' ... well, I had a feeling we might have to get away quick somewhere tonight, so I put these clothes on and slept in 'em. Reckon you had the same idea, being as I expect you don't usually sleep in all your clothes, do you?"

Jacob felt himself reddening and was glad it was still dark.

"Come on, Sarah," he said. "There's nothing more to be done here and the sun will be up before long, so let's go home."

When Mrs Tucker arrived in the kitchen the following morning, she was surprised to see that neither Jacob nor Sarah had risen yet. Shaking her head at this proof that they were engaged in questionable if not downright immoral behavior, she set the kettle boiling for tea.

Eventually Sarah came downstairs, to be met with a disapproving frown.

"What time do you call this, girl?" she demanded of Sarah.

"Sorry, Mrs Tucker." Sarah yawned and glanced at Jacob, who had followed her down the stairs, confirming Mrs Tucker's worst suspicions. "Do you want a boiled egg for breakfast, Mr Silver?"

"Yes, I would. But a cup of tea first, please, Mrs Tucker."

She poured it silently, while Sarah put the egg on to boil. Mrs Tucker's eyes darted from Sarah to Jacob, but after a minute or so, her desire to gossip overcame any suspicions she might have had about their nocturnal activities.

"I come through the town this morning," she said, "being as I don't fancy walkin' that footpath any more where that poor girl was killed. And I heard people sayin' that London police inspector took Nathaniel Martyn away last night and he's locked up in Oxford jail now. They're sayin' he killed his own pa and that Sally Wright as well; can you believe that?

"And Jerome Mead, he's back in Witney today, tellin' anybody that'll listen that he knew he'd never be blamed for Mr Martyn's death, and shame on them as believed it. What do you think of that, Mr Silver?"

"I think," Jacob said, putting his cup down, "that a great many things may be changing in this town as a result of Thomas Martyn's death. But some things, such as human nature, will always remain the same."

Jacob didn't feel any urge to go into town, reasoning that whatever rumors were flying around – and he knew there were many – he and Sarah knew far more details and explanations.

And it suddenly didn't seem such an urgent matter to speak to Rexford about Martyn's will, now that Nathaniel was unlikely to ever benefit from it. So he pretended it was a perfectly normal day, going into his workshop once he had finished his breakfast, and working on a malfunctioning carriage clock.

Before he started, however, he took Martyn's pocket watch from the bag in his pocket and placed it on the workbench where he could admire it. He had no idea whether Sarah would be allowed to keep it, since there were Charlotte Worth's legitimate children to consider, but at least she would have the temporary satisfaction of knowing her great-grandfather had been the original owner.

It was nearly midday when the message he had been half expecting came, in the form of a messenger boy, a little older and a little cleaner than the one Dr Sheridan employed. He rapped on the door and when Jacob opened it, he stood to attention and delivered his message, which he had obviously memorized.

"Mr Rexford wishes you and Miss Simm to attend his office when it is convenient for you to do so, and to bring the watch," he said. Then, unbending a little, he added, "He says you'll know what he means. Says could you come about half two this afternoon, Mr Silver, if you're not too busy."

"Certainly," Jacob said. "You may tell Mr Rexford we both will be there at half two. Thank you."

He gave the boy his expected tip for delivering the message and went into the kitchen, where Sarah was on her knees, raking the ashes and cinders out of the stove. Her hands were dirty and a small cloud of coal dust rose around her.

"Mr Rexford wants to see us both this afternoon, Sarah," he said. "So I think we may have been right about Thomas Martyn's will."

"Oh, no," Sarah said, sitting back on her heels. "Oh, Mr Silver, I don't know as I want anythin' from them. And what about Mrs Worth? She's expectin' me to start working for her today."

"She can hardly still expect that after the events of last night. And let's see what Mr Rexford has to say before you take any decisions."

"Yes, sir." She got to her feet and dusted her hands on her apron. "I'll get cleaned up and then do us some soup."

"And I have been asked to bring the watch with me," Jacob said. "I'll also take those portraits Nathaniel was so eager to dispose of. That should answer any number of questions."

It was precisely two-thirty when Jacob and Sarah presented themselves at John Rexford's office. Jacob was wearing a spotless shirt, freshly ironed trousers and his fine wool coat, and Sarah was in her best dress, coat and the hat she normally wore only to church, the black ribbon now removed. They had walked together to Church Green, ignoring the curious looks thrown their direction. A pin-stripe suited clerk ushered them into the inner chamber, his disdain showing clearly. Jacob smiled at him pleasantly.

He expected that they would be the only people there, and was startled to see Charlotte Worth already seated, along with an older woman dressed completely in black. Her face was lined and there were dark circles under her eyes, as if she hadn't slept for several nights.

"May I present Mrs Evangeline Martyn, and her daughter, Mrs Charlotte Worth," Rexford said. "Mr Jacob Silver and Miss Sarah Simm. I thank you all for coming here today, especially you, Mrs Martyn. I know that in the normal course of events you would have been at home, since you are in mourning, but it is important for all of you to be present."

Evangeline Martyn's tired eyes were focused on Sarah; Jacob doubted that she was hearing Rexford's words or seeing anything else in the room. He fingered the portraits in his pocket as he bowed politely to both women, amused to see that Mrs Worth gave no indication they had previously met.

Nor did either woman acknowledge the fact that their son and brother had been arrested during the night for the murders of his father and an innocent girl. Since Carey had certainly informed them, he gave them credit for fortitude in the face of that appalling news.

"Mrs Martyn, Mrs Worth," he said.

"Ma'am," Sarah said, making what might have been a half curtsey to Mrs Martyn and simply bobbing her head to Charlotte Worth.

They both took seats facing Rexford, who folded his hands and gazed at them.

"I will attempt to come straight to the point," he said, "although the situation has been vastly complicated by the arrest of Nathaniel Martyn last night. I daresay you know of that?"

"Yes, sir," Jacob said.

"However, Miss Simm's position remains the same. The family are aware of the terms of Thomas Martyn's will, so I shall share only the portion which refers to her. But first, a few questions."

Sarah sat up straight, her chin high, as Rexford addressed her.

"What was your mother's name, Miss Simm?"

"Anne Porter, sir, afore she was married to James Simm."

"And was she a maid in the Martyn household?"

"Yes, sir."

"Did she ever allude to Frederick Martyn, the elder son of the house?"

"Allude, sir?"

"Speak of him, that is."

"Not as such, sir. Except she did say once or twice that if I'd been a boy, I'd have been called Fred. I thought it were a joke, like."

Charlotte Worth gasped. Her mother nodded slightly.

"Did she ever give you reason to think your natural father was Frederick Martyn?"

"No, sir. Not at all."

"She kept her word, then," Evangeline Martyn said. Her voice was hoarse, as if she'd been crying.

"Mama," Mrs Worth said. "Don't distress yourself. It's obvious this girl and the Jew are conspiring together to discredit our family."

"I'm not distressed, Charlotte," her mother said sharply. "And it would be difficult to discredit our family any more than we have been over the past few days. Annie Porter was one of the best maids I ever had, a charming girl, and Frederick was deeply in love with her."

"Mama, you know that's not true."

"Be quiet, Charlotte. You were only a girl of fourteen; what would you have known?"

Charlotte compressed her lips.

"Nothing would have come of it, of course," Mrs Martyn continued, "but when we learned she was with child, Thomas insisted that I dismiss her. He didn't know Frederick was the father. Annie admitted he was – as I had suspected, having seen them together – but I asked her to keep quiet about it, and she promised she would. I hoped I would be able to do something to help her. Then Frederick fell ill, and just before the child was born – a girl Annie called Sarah – he died of typhoid."

She swallowed hard and Jacob knew that Frederick had been her favorite child. As one who had also watched his child die, he felt a deep sympathy toward her.

"When did your husband learn that Frederick had left a daughter?" Rexford asked her gently.

"Not until a few days ago. Nathaniel told him. I'm not sure how Nathaniel found out or when he learned it; perhaps Frederick had confided in him years earlier. Nathaniel said he and his father were arguing about something and Thomas said he wasn't half the man his brother had been. Nathaniel lost his temper and said Frederick hadn't been as good and pure as Thomas thought he was. And he told him why.

"Thomas was furious at first, but after he had spoken with me and confirmed it, he calmed down. He confessed that Annie had appealed to him some three years earlier, after her husband had died, and he had turned her away. He hadn't told me. He said he would not have done that if he had known her older child was Frederick's daughter."

Sarah sat motionless.

"And later that day," Rexford said, "Thomas Martyn came to me and changed his will. The bulk of the estate still went to Nathaniel as the surviving son, with generous provisions for his wife and daughter. But he added two bequests, which I will read now."

"Just a minute, Mr Rexford," Charlotte said. "There is no proof at all that this girl is Frederick's daughter, if indeed one exists. My brother Nathaniel and I discussed it before his ... misfortune ... and we doubt her claims are true."

Before the solicitor could respond, Jacob took the portraits from his pocket and laid them on Rexford's desk, where Charlotte could see them clearly.

"Perhaps these will convince you, Mrs Worth," he said. "Miss Simm resembles her father to a great degree. And a bit of further proof – Nathaniel Martyn pawned these portraits some time ago but made no effort to redeem them. Almost as if he did not want anyone who had known Frederick well to see them. And if there is no connection between Sarah Simm and yourself, why did you seek her out and order her – out of all the housemaids in Witney – to come and work for you? I think you wanted to see for yourself if she might be your niece."

Charlotte's eyes shot daggers in Jacob's direction, but she said nothing.

"May I proceed now, Mrs Worth?" Rexford asked. When there was no reply, he opened a document and read from it.

"To Sarah, the natural daughter of my son Frederick, I bequeath the gold watch my father received after the battle of Waterloo. I have given it to the clock repairer Jacob Silver, residing in Corn Street, for safekeeping, and I hereby instruct him to find Frederick's daughter, confirm her identity and present the watch to her. I also bequeath to Sarah, natural daughter of my son Frederick, an annual sum of one hundred pounds, to commence on my death."

Sarah's eyes grew wide. Jacob knew it was a pittance to Thomas Martyn but a fortune to her, several times as much as a housemaid could ever expect to earn in a year. As for the watch, it, too was valuable, but in sentiment as well as monetary terms.

"Invested wisely, an annual income of hundred pounds will allow you to set up your own small household when you are a little older, Miss Simm," Rexford said.

"Oh, no, I won't do that, sir," Sarah said quickly. "Mr Silver's said I can stop with him as long as I want to, and as he's the only one who's been good to me since Ma died, that's what I'll do."

She transferred her attention to Mrs Martyn.

"Thank you, ma'am, for them – those – kind words about Ma. It means a lot to me, knowin' she was appreciated and that Frederick loved her. And Mrs Worth, thank you for offerin' me a position, but I won't be takin' it up."

Charlotte was making an obvious effort to control herself, and Jacob tried to keep from laughing.

"I shall make arrangements for the funds to be paid to you, Miss Simm," Rexford said. "And advise you about investing them, if that is your wish."

"Thank you, sir."

"And here is your great-grandfather's watch," Jacob said, laying it on the desk. Sarah took it and held it lightly in her hand. He remembered how she had clutched the watch the day she had returned it to him, and smiled. "You will note, Mr Rexford, that I have now fulfilled my obligation to Thomas Martyn."

"It will be duly noted," Rexford said.

"Thank you, Mr Silver," Sarah said.

"You are the most extraordinary person," Charlotte said in disgust. "You'd rather stay in that Corn Street hovel, slaving away for this heretic, than live in comfort in Oxford?"

"That's right, ma'am, I would," Sarah said.

Charlotte stood up, gave her a last, disdainful glance and swept out of the room, her black skirts billowing behind her. Her mother moved more slowly, bestowing a tentative smile on Sarah.

"You are a spirited girl," she said. "Although it appears you are my granddaughter, I doubt we shall see much of each other in future. I'm sure you understand why. But I wish you all the best."

"Thank you, ma'am. I understand."

"Look after the watch. Someday you may be able to pass it to your own son."

"Yes, ma'am. I hope I shall."

Evangeline Martyn left the room and Jacob looked at Sarah.

"Come, Sarah," he said. "Let's go home."

A few weeks later, Jacob was walking down Corn Street on a damp afternoon when he saw a large delivery van pulled up in front of one of the houses. It was a slightly grander one than his own, and he knew it had been empty for several months. Men were carrying chests and pieces of furniture inside, and Jacob deduced that someone was taking possession.

He paused and watched with interest, trying to gauge something of the identities and characters of the new occupants. Judging from the belongings he could see, they had a moderate income, an interest in books, had either traveled or had relations in India, and weren't planning to cook much.

He turned toward the town and nearly ran into Inspector Carey, who had emerged from the far side of the van.

"Good afternoon, Mr Silver," Carey said. "What have you observed?"

"Good afternoon, sir," Jacob said, trying to hide his surprise. "It appears new occupants are moving into that house, and I confess I was curious as to who they might be. So far there are few clues, but they seem to be interested in reading and foreign lands, if not domestic activities. Are you in Witney again as part of your official duties, Inspector?"

"You may say that. It has been decided that in the wake of the recent events here, Witney needs more policing than two officers can provide. I have been posted to the town, to take up my duties next week, and I am looking forward to the challenge."

"And you are going to be living here?" Jacob gestured toward the house.

"That's right, Mr Silver. You and I are to be neighbors."

Jacob wasn't entirely sure the idea appealed to him, but there was little he could do about it.

"Is Miss Simm still in your household?" Carey asked.

"Yes, she is."

"Her new-found riches did not induce her to leave, then?"

Jacob didn't bother to inquire how Carey had learned of Sarah's change of fortune. Either Rexford had said something or more likely, Nathaniel had, out of spite.

"I don't think they qualify as riches, precisely, but I doubted they would make her leave. She is like a stray kitten who has found a warm hearth and is now reluctant to venture very far from it."

"A good description," Carey said, nodding. "I believe you have a rare gem there, Mr Silver."

"Yes, Jacob said. "I believe I do."

Thank you for reading *Tools of the Trade*. If you enjoyed it, please tell your friends and leave a review!

Cynthia E. Hurst is also the author of two light-hearted mystery series set in present-day Seattle, the R&P Labs Mysteries and the Zukie Merlino Mysteries.

Mossfire (R&P Labs Mysteries 1)
Sweetwater (R&P Labs Mysteries 2)
Shellshock (R&P Labs Mysteries 3)
Angelwood (R&P Labs Mysteries 4)
Boneflower (R&P Labs Mysteries 5)
Childproof (R&P Labs Mysteries 6)
Dreamwheel (R&P Labs Mysteries 7)
Icefox (R&P Labs Mysteries 8)
Shotglass (R&P Labs Mysteries 9)
Pushover (R&P Labs Mysteries 10)
Bedrock (R&P Labs Mysteries 11)
Uprooted (R&P Labs Mysteries 12)
Four by Five (R&P Labs Mysteries Short Stories)

Zukie's Burglar (Zukie Merlino Mysteries 1)
Zukie's Witness (Zukie Merlino Mysteries 2)
Zukie's Suspect (Zukie Merlino Mysteries 3)
Zukie's Detective (Zukie Merlino Mysteries 4)
Zukie's Alibi (Zukie Merlino Mysteries 5)
Zukie's Evidence (Zukie Merlino Mysteries 6)
Zukie's Promise (Zukie Merlino Mysteries 7)
Zukie's Trail (Zukie Merlino Mysteries 8)
Zukie's Ghost (Zukie Merlino Mysteries 9)

Printed in Great Britain
by Amazon

38722073R00126